LESS
is
MORE

Real TV
TAKE THREE

LESS
is MORE

WENDY LAWTON

MOODY PUBLISHERS
CHICAGO

Library of Congress Cataloging-in-Publication Data

Lawton, Wendy.
    Less is more / Wendy Lawton.
       p. cm. — (Real TV—real transformations series ; take 3)
    Summary: Having gaining weight after her father's death, sixteen-year-old Abby goes on a reality television program and works, with the help of her friends, family, and faith, to meet her health and fitness goals.
    ISBN-13: 978-0-8024-5415-7
    [1. Weight control—Fiction. 2. Reality television programs—Fiction. 3. Self-realization—Fiction. 4. Grief—Fiction. 5. Christian life—Fiction.] I. Title.

PZ7.L4425Le 2005
[Fic]—dc22

2004028015

ISBN: 0-8024-5415-1
EAN/ISBN-13: 0-8024-5415-7

1 3 5 7 9 10 8 6 4 2

For April

*Since that very first day you befriended
a timid fellow third-grader who walked into your classroom
at St. John's on South Van Ness Avenue in San Francisco,
you've been a kindred spirit and a forever friend.*

Contents

RealTV

Acknowledgments

Special thanks to The Learning Channel, Style Network, and BBC television programs that spawned the concept for the *Real TV* series. For *Less is More,* I was inspired by Discovery Health's *National Body Challenge.* The creators of these programs —despite the fun and fluff—actually take the concept of makeover much deeper.

And, as always, big thanks to Andrew McGuire and the incomparable editorial and design team at Moody Publishers and to my agent, Janet Grant. I appreciate the patience of my family as I endured my own *Less is More* sort of quest during the writing of this book—I wanted to experience the challenge right along with Abby.

Changes

1

"**Mom.**" Abby waved her hand over the dressing room door. "Are you out there?"

"Right here."

"Can you come here?" Abby waited until her mom tapped on the door before she opened it a crack. "I can't even get these jeans over my hips. I don't get this sizing."

"Want me to come in and have a look?"

"No!" Abby didn't mean to snap, but there she stood, jeans jammed midthigh. Saddlebags of dimpled flesh bulged out on both sides, hanging over the strangulating waistband. The sight disgusted her. "I mean, that's okay. I just need you to—" A peal of laughter sounded from the dressing room a couple of doors down, followed by whispers and giggles. Must have been a group of girls shopping together.

"What do you need?" Mom asked.

Abby opened the door a little wider and whispered, "I think I need the next largest size. Not the faded ones, the dark ones." She looked back over her shoulder at the mirror and sighed. "Can you also bring the size above that?"

"Sweetheart, let me in," Mom said as she pushed on the door.

"Just a minute." Abby tugged at the jeans, pushing them to the floor where she could step out of them. She kicked them to one side and slid her worn carpenter pants up to her waist. "Okay, come in."

Mom smiled as she looked at the crumpled pile of jeans on the floor. "See? You really do need your favorite dressing room maid to hang and fold as you go." She reached down and picked up the last pair, smoothing them out. "Let's try another store."

"Okay, but I really liked that last pair of pants. I just need a little bigger size."

Mom folded the jeans without making eye contact. "Unfortunately, this store stops at that size, honey."

"What do you mean?" She watched her mother pick up another pair of jeans from the floor.

"This store only handles junior sizes. They stop with this size." Mom continued to fold.

Abby didn't know what to say. She knew that about this store. At least she'd once known that. Okay. She'd put on weight since the move. Cece's cooking. She hadn't dared step on a scale. Especially since she'd spent most of the last three months snacking while watching television and snacking while reading and snacking while writing e-mails and snacking while sending IMs to her old friends in Suwanee and, well, snacking while staring out the window. But when you didn't know a single person in the entire city besides your mother and grandmother, what else could you do?

"I hate these stores."

"You're just unfamiliar with them," Mom soothed in her best encouraging voice.

"Yeah, I'm unfamiliar, but I also hate them." She looked at herself in the mirror and hated the sound of her voice—almost as much as she hated her reflection. Who *was* that looking back at her?

"But don't you love the excitement of shopping in a big city? The metro culture and all that?"

"Mom, except for Guess and Gap and Nike, there are mostly old-people stores here. What teen can afford Prada, Versace, or Louis Vuitton? San Francisco is not exactly the most happening place, you know."

"Maybe part of that is because we are shopping on a weekday." Mom stacked the clothes. "Ready to go?"

They walked out of the dressing room area empty-handed. Abby didn't even acknowledge the "how did you do?" question from the dressing room attendant.

"We didn't find what we were after," Mom said. "But thanks for your help."

They took the elevator down to the first floor and wove their way through the counters and shoppers and out onto the street.

"Can we just go get something to drink? I think I'm sick of shopping."

"Sure. I could use a cup of coffee. Are you up for a mocha?"

"Okay."

"Maybe it will refresh us enough to get back to the task of finding you some cute school clothes."

"Cute?" Abby didn't mean to sound cynical, but she was already sick of the whole clothes thing.

"Oh, Abby," Mom said. "I know I use the wrong words, and I know shopping is no fun when you can't find the right styles and . . . "

"You know it's not about style, Mom. It's about size." The words tumbled out. "I need to face facts. I've been living in a cocoon—in a fog. How could I have put on enough weight to change more than two sizes?" Just the thought of it made Abby want to cry.

Mom opened the door of the Starbucks. "Go get us a table. I'll get our coffees."

Abby sat down at the small table in the corner by the window. Her chest hurt. Was she having a heart attack? *Don't be stupid. You don't need to become a hypochondriac on top of everything else.*

"Here we are." Mom set the drinks on the table. "I'll get napkins. You didn't want something sweet to go with the coffee?"

Abby shook her head, pressing her lips together. She needed to shake this mood. It was one of the few days she and Mom had stirred to go out together. Was she going to let her disappointment ruin everything? Mom didn't deserve it.

She looked at her mother, standing to the side so a businessman could get his cream. Why couldn't she be slender like Mom? Mom looked as pretty as ever—her

dark brown hair and blue eyes setting off a great complexion. Cece always called it Snow White coloring.

Ever since Dad . . .

Abby stopped midthought. She still couldn't bring
herself to say—or even *think*—that word. Ever since she
and her mother had moved to San Francisco to live
with Cece, Mom had hardly been able to eat. Abby was
the exact opposite. She couldn't seem to get enough.
Emotional eating. Dr. Phil had a guest on his show last
month who called it that.

"Here you are." Mom laid a napkin down on the
table for her.

"Did you ever come here when you were my age?"
There. Change the subject.

"Starbucks?" Mom laughed. "They didn't have anything like Starbucks when I was growing up."

Abby made her silly "duh" face. "I know that. I
meant Union Square."

"Sure. This is where Cece always took me shopping.
Here or else Market Street. Sometimes my dad joined
our Easter shopping trip. It was a big deal because we'd
go into the Emporium and watch the baby chicks
hatch."

"Chicks hatch?"

"I don't know if they still do it, but they used to
have an Easter display with eggs in something like a
showcase that hatched into tiny chicks right before our
eyes."

"Not real live chicks . . . "

"Uh-huh. They were fertile eggs, and it must have
been warm like an incubator and—"

"Oh, Mom. Can you imagine what the ASPCA
would say about that these days?"

"I don't know. I guess I never thought about it. But how we loved to watch." Mom seemed to sort of drift off. The childhood memories must have been easier than thinking about Dad. "Cece always made me dress up for shopping—gloves and all—and we'd take the bus downtown. We'd stand there in the store and watch the baby chicks for the longest time."

Mom juggled her coffee from hand to hand. She didn't complain about hot coffee in paper cups this time, but Abby had heard the objection enough times to know what Mom was thinking as she finally put the cup on the table to let it cool some.

Abby savored the chocolaty taste of her drink.

Things changed so fast. No one even saw it coming. If she and Mom hadn't moved to San Francisco, she'd be shopping with Jen and Michelle at the Mall of Georgia. School clothes shopping with best friends worked so much better, because they'd drag you all over the place until you found something that worked. Jen would know exactly what to do to camouflage all this weight. She'd drape something or wrap something or help find an accessory that would pull the eyes away from the bulging areas.

"You look like you're miles away," Mom said.

"I guess I was." Twenty-five-hundred miles, to be exact.

"So what were you thinking?"

"About Jen and Michelle."

Mom waited for her to go on.

Abby loved her mother. She did not want to make her feel bad. What could she say? Shopping is more fun with girlfriends? That she'd much rather shop at a modern mall than downtown San Francisco?

"I was thinking that if we were shopping at the Mall of Georgia, Jen would bug us to do the bungee-swing thing. We'd finally give in . . . "

"You wouldn't," Mom said in *that* voice as she set her coffee down.

"Not for reals. But we'd get in line as if we were going to until Jen would finally let us off the hook. She was more scared than we were, but she always had to force herself to at least consider doing something daring."

"You really miss them." It was not a question.

Abby nodded. "You miss your friends, don't you?"

"Of course."

Two college-age girls walked in carrying artists' black portfolio cases. They wedged their cases between the window and a chair and walked up to the counter to order. Abby liked the way the larger girl dressed. If she could find a V-neck sweater like that—not too short —it might help smooth over some of the problem areas.

"Abby?"

"Oh, sorry, Mom."

"I know this move and all these changes have been hard on you." She bit the corner of her mouth. "Maybe we should have stayed put . . . stayed with our friends, but I couldn't seem to get away from memories no matter how hard I tried."

Abby didn't say anything. It was the same for her, but memories were good and helped her stay close to Dad.

"I thought it would be a good idea to get away— new faces, new places . . ."

"But I loved the old places, old faces," Abby said.

Mom pulled the cardboard sleeve off her coffee and opened the lid to take a drink. "I'll confess. I felt battered by sorrow. The thought of coming home to my own mom sounded so good. To eat in her kitchen, to show you my old city . . . I don't know . . ." Mom ran a hand through her hair.

"Well, I like being with Cece." And she did. When Abby was a baby she couldn't manage to say "grandma," but she heard Dad call her grandmother by name —Elsie. Mom had said it wasn't long until Abby started saying her own version of Elsie—Cece. The name stuck.

"So do I." Mom began tidying the table.

"Are you about ready to go?" Abby asked, slurping the last noisy bit of her mocha through a coffee stirrer.

"Uh-huh." She stuffed the napkins and the cardboard sleeve into her cup. "About all these changes, Abby . . . nothing is forever."

"You don't have to tell me that, Mom." Abby made a soft snorting sound as she got up to put their stuff into the trash. "That's the understatement of the year."

Mom nodded her agreement. "But what I meant was that we still have our house in Suwanee, and there's nothing to say we won't end up back there. We can pretend this is an adventure—a new start. Okay?"

An adventure? Abby didn't know how to respond to that. "Let's try one more store." Abby dropped her voice. "See that girl over against the window . . . the one in the dark sweater? I'd like to try to find a sweater like that."

Finding a sweater that actually fit was about all the adventure Abby could take at this time. Losing her dad, losing her friends, losing her church, and losing the body shape she was accustomed to was all she could handle right now. Who was she kidding? It was way more than she could handle.

In just a week, school would be starting back home at North Gwinnett High. She wondered who would have her old locker between Jen's and Michelle's. Maybe when she got back to Cece's, her friends would be online and she could chat for a while. The three-hour time difference between California and Georgia made it tough to connect sometimes.

As she walked toward Macy's West beside her mother, Abby knew that she needed to make some real live friends.

❋   ❋   ❋

"Mmmm, that smells good." Mom slid into the chair to the right of Cece. "Like something you used to make when I was little."

They always ate in the oak-lined dining room—three places set at the end of a heavy walnut table that could have comfortably seated eight or ten. Cece sat at the head, Mom on the right, Abby on the left. Abby wondered what it had been like after Grandpa died when Cece had eaten alone at the head of the table. How lonely.

But tonight Cece was happy as she finished preparing dinner, talking to Abby's mother the whole time. "It's Tater Tot Casserole. I gave you the recipe, Karen. Remember? I got it when you were in . . . was that third grade or fourth grade? Let's see . . . you had that teacher who came from Indiana. Remember?"

"It was third grade, Mom."

"That's right. I should have remembered. You had that purple sweater vest you loved." Cece stirred something in the kitchen. Abby could hear the spoon scraping against the metal of the pot. Her grandmother often remembered dates by what grade Mom had been in and what she'd worn.

Cece put a 9 x 12 pan on the table. "Anyway, the PTA came out with a cookbook based on the best-ever potluck recipes. You loved this one—all cheesy."

Mom laughed. "Abby, believe it or not, this is comfort food for me. How I used to love these kinds of dinners."

Abby looked at the dish. She hated it when food got all mixed together. At home in Suwanee, Mom used to laugh when she talked about her mother's cooking style and regale them with funny Cece-cuisine stories. Apparently, when Cece was a young wife—before she and Grandpa had enough money to buy fancy packaged food—Mom remembered that her mother used to make bread from scratch and serve plain vegetables and whatever small portions of meat they could afford.

Abby smiled. There was nothing quite like the advent of TV to ruin good healthy food in those days. In the sixties, as Grandpa began to move up in the family business, Cece finally had money to buy all the advertised-on-TV designer foods. Mom would laugh as she recounted the lineup: Spam, Hamburger Helper, Velveeta Cheese, Bosco, and Cheese Whiz on Hi Ho Crackers. Brand-name cuisine.

Abby laughed every time her mom told the stories. Even the names sounded funny to her. Abby looked at the food on the table. Somehow it didn't seem all that funny now.

Here in Cece's house, Abby had to remember to take out the trash every single night, because it was stuffed to the brim with bulky boxes and packages that took up space. Cece liked nothing better than combining packaged, prepared foods into some kind of concoction with a perky name.

"And for dessert I have that Jell-O you love with the coconut, miniature marshmallows, and Cool Whip."

Mom laughed and bumped Abby's foot under the table. Her laughter sounded good to Abby. Mom had rarely laughed in the last seven months. If it took a weird mishmash of food to make her mom laugh, then let the feast begin.

Abby thought about her jeans fiasco today. She knew this kind of food wasn't helping. Cece's three major food groups seemed to be carbs, fat, and sugar. Back in Suwanee, Mom used to steam vegetables, broil meat or fish, or do fun things like pasta primavera. Healthy stuff.

Fat lot of good it did to focus on healthy eating, though. Dad had still died of a heart attack. And all anybody could say was, "But he was so young, so healthy." It hadn't seemed to matter. The doctor explained that it was a defect in the aorta or something. *Massive* was the word they kept using.

"Abby, aren't you going to have some casserole?" Cece waited, spoon in hand.

"Might as well." It hardly mattered what you ate anyway. When she lifted her fork to her mouth, she found it actually tasted pretty good despite the lumpy, crusty appearance—sort of a cross between hash browns, beef Stroganoff, and macaroni and cheese.

"Your grandpa used to say this kind of food really sticks to the ribs." Cece handed her a biscuit—the kind that popped out of a refrigerated can, ready for the oven.

By the time Abby stood up to clear the table she felt stuffed. Grandpa knew what he was talking about—this stuff stuck to the ribs, all right. If one could still feel one's ribs, that is.

"Abigail," her mom called from the living room, "Want to watch *Less is More* with me?"

"Sure, give me a minute to waddle in there." That was supposed to be a joke, but somehow it didn't seem so funny tonight. She and Mom had gotten addicted to the reality fitness program last season, and it was still fun to watch the reruns. The show picked six overweight, out-of-shape people and put them on a regimen and followed them for twelve two-week segments. As the weeks passed, you got to know the people and their struggles and you began to root for them. Each contestant had a personal trainer and a personal food coach chosen for him—so it was a team thing. "I've already seen this one, but maybe some of the wisdom will sink in," Abby said.

Cece joined them as they watched. Each contestant had to compete in a footrace together for this episode before his weigh-in. All the participants were together only twice during the season. The rest of the time, each team had their own camera crew that followed them at home. The competition and interaction made this episode fun.

As the race sequence ran, Abby decided it felt a lot more comfortable watching from the couch than straining to finish a five-kilometer race. But as she watched the hard work and the pounds lost, she wished she could do the same thing. Somehow she needed to take control of her life—or at least one part of her life. As the episode closed, she found herself praying, *Help me,*

Father. I want to find my way again. I may not win a race,
but help me at least get back in the running.

"Are you going up already?" Mom asked as Abby
kissed her.

"Not to bed yet, but I want to go online and read a
little before bed. Good night Cece." She blew a kiss to
her grandmother as she headed upstairs.

"Dear Dad," she typed once she was back in her
room with the door closed. "Time for another e-mail.
Okay, I know you no longer check your e-mail, but a
girl can pretend, can't she? LOL."

Abby found some strange satisfaction in writing
these e-mails to her dad. His address still worked at
AmericasMart. At least she assumed it did—her e-mail
never got returned as undeliverable. Sometimes she'd
picture him—still sitting at that big wooden desk in the
leasing office—reading her e-mail.

If only.

"I can't believe I'm actually living in Cece's house,"
she wrote. "You used to call it an old mausoleum (I
hope I spelled that right). It's definitely nothing like our
house in Suwanee—all sunny and new. I think Mom
likes sleeping in the bed she slept in when she was my
age. Maybe it helps her miss you less."

Abby picked up her can of Coke to take a drink. Coke
made her think of Atlanta. "Okay. I'm not going to go
into the whole 'missing you' thing again. That gets old
quick, doesn't it? I'm determined to try to get through
this, Dad. I guess it's kind of like Mom and her adventure. LOL. As if moving in with your seventy-something
mother is an adventure, but as you used to say, 'Any port
in a storm.'

"Speaking of ports in a storm, I need to get busy and

make some new friends. I keep remembering what you always said about working at friendship. You called it being proactive about seeking friends and keeping them. Did you know that I had no idea what you meant by that word for the longest time?"

"Abby, " Mom called from downstairs. "Pick up the phone."

Nobody called her in California. She lifted the phone. "Hello?"

"Abby? This is Tracy Mathews. I'm one of the Phys Ed teachers at Emerson. Everyone calls me Coach Mathews."

"Hi," Abby said tentatively. None of her teachers at North Gwinnett had ever called her at home.

"Besides working at school, I'm a new adviser of the high school group at your grandmother's church." She paused. "We're having an end-of-summer party to kick off our new school year and would love to have you come."

She was just writing to Dad about needing new friends. Could this be her chance? "When is it?"

"We'll meet at seven on Friday night. At the Bistro."

"The Bistro?"

"That's what we call the basement at church. We've fixed it up to be kind of like a European bistro."

"It sounds like fun. Do I bring something? Does it cost anything?"

"No cost. Just bring something to snack on. We'll have pizza and drinks." She paused. "Oh, yes. Bring a souvenir or a photo from this summer for a show-and-tell. Something to help you tell us what you did over the summer."

"Okay."

After they said good-bye, Abby went back to her e-mail. "Gotta run, Dad. I'm going to do my best to make some friends. Now we just have to work on Mom." Before she hit the Send button, she added the following: "I miss you so much that it hurts. I know I said I wouldn't go on and on about it, but I can't help it. You know the worst thing? If all this was a big mistake and you were somehow still alive, like on a business trip or something and you came back, you'd never recognize me. I don't know how it happened, but I've put on weight—tons of weight. I totally disgust myself."

She stopped typing for a minute while a smile crinkled her face. She typed, "I know exactly what you would say if you could reply to my e-mail. 'Don't sweat it. God may not be done with you yet, but He loves you, and I love you just the way you are.'" Yep. That's exactly what he'd say. She added her sig line and pushed the Send button.

Nicknames

2

Abby woke early on Friday morning. What could she take to the group that would tell a little about her summer but not reveal all the gruesome details? As she walked downstairs, she ran her fingers over the embossed relief Lincrusta on the walls of the stairway. The bumpiness reminded her of long years ago when she was a toddler visiting Cece and held the walls to steady herself.

She liked this old San Francisco Victorian. Cece claimed it had the finest oak staircase in the whole Sunset District. You'd think the location would be enough—it was only six houses down Eleventh Avenue from where Eleventh intersected Golden Gate Park—but it was the house itself that Abby appreciated. She always felt as if she'd stepped into another era when she visited Cece. Only now she wasn't visiting; she lived here. It was not Suwanee, but . . .

"Morning." Mom sat at the table in the kitchen with a mug of coffee. "You're up early."

"You too." Abby scooted out a chair and joined her mother at the table. How could her mom look pretty in the morning? Maybe it was her complexion. It didn't need any makeup to glow. Because her hair was dark brown, Mom never looked washed out. What happened to those genes? Abby sure didn't get them. Abby's blonde hair and brown eyes looked great when she had a tan—or at least a healthy glow to her skin, since tanning was a no-no these days—but she'd barely been out this summer. Washed out. That's what she was. Washed out and fat. What a combination.

"I was just thinking about the house," Abby said, not wanting to go into the self-loathing thing with Mom.

"Me too. It feels so comforting to me." Mom put her cup down. "Want some hot chocolate?"

"Sure. Who'd ever guess you'd need to warm up on a morning in August?"

Mom got up to put a pan of milk on the stove. "Summer in San Francisco. Brrrr."

"It sure is different from Georgia, isn't it?" Abby wondered if she'd ever wear shorts again. The Sunset had the best weather in the city, but when those fingers of fog drifted over the hills, it felt downright chilly.

"Everyone in the city quotes Mark Twain. He was

supposed to have said that the coldest winter he ever spent was the summer in San Francisco. I don't think he really said it, but the sentiment is not far off." Mom stood at the old stove and shaved chocolate into the hot milk. "Cece is amazing in what she coaxes out of her garden despite this climate."

Like most San Francisco Victorian homes, Cece's was narrow, butting neighboring houses on both sides, but the lot was deep. If you went down into the basement and out the back door, you'd be in another world. Her garden had flowers of every color and kind from wisteria and geraniums to hydrangeas and roses. Abby loved the garden.

"So what's your plan for today?" Mom asked as she put a mug of hot chocolate on the table.

"I'm going to the youth group at Cece's church for dinner, and I need to take a souvenir or a photo to share—something that tells about summer vacation. I can't figure out what to take." She took a sip of the chocolate. *Mmmm. Could a person ever get enough chocolate?*

Mom thought for a minute. "What about that photo of us rolling down the door on the moving van?"

"Perfect." A picture said it all—the end of an era.

＊　　　＊　　　＊

That night, when Abby walked into the church basement she saw that it did look like a bistro. Or at least what she figured a bistro might look like. The walls were painted a mellow and aged kind of mottled yellow and were hung with red-framed French and Italian posters. Instead of the usual church basement long tables and folding chairs, there were round tables with black-and-white-checkered plastic tablecloths, surrounded by old restaurant-type chairs. In the center of each table was a raffia-covered bottle with two or three colorful Gerbera daisies. Cute.

A group of kids milled around, looking out of place and uncomfortable. That was pretty much how Abby felt. She tugged on her sweater but stopped herself from sizing up the group to see if she was the most overweight girl at the meeting.

"Sit down, everyone," said one guy who stood up from a group of five kids who sat at the table nearest the counter. He looked to be president or leader of the youth group—maybe a senior. He oozed self-confidence.

Abby found a seat toward the back. Another girl, probably a freshman, pulled out a chair and sat down, mumbling, "May I?" Abby nodded, but there was no time to speak.

"Welcome, everyone, to the kickoff of a new school year and a new start here at the Bistro. I'm Damian, better known as Bistro Boss." He smiled and pointed to the girl next to him. "This is Andrea, vice president, who takes care of everything I don't have time to worry about. I call her the Bistro Babe."

Is this a church youth group? Abby could see already that the way things were done in the city was way different from back home. A few kids leaned in and whispered to their tablemates.

"Our secretary is Jamie, but she spends more time hopping around than actually taking readable minutes. So she is the Bistro Bunny." Jamie got up and took a bow. "And our faithful treasurer, Trina, takes care of the

30

money, so we call her the Bistro Bank." Trina made a face.

"But that's more than enough Bistro Bs. Our program chairman is Parker, and we just call him Park, 'cause that's what we've called him since kindergarten." The guy named Parker stood up and smiled, sort of waving his hand. He seemed a little uncomfortable.

"By now," Damian continued, "you may have realized that we're not like your run-of-the-mill church group. And that's a good thing, kiddies." He pointed to the kitchen where three adults were organizing food. "Oops. I forgot to introduce you to our support staff. Preach and Shelly?"

The three who'd been working behind the counter came out.

"This is our youth pastor, Pastor Doug, and his wife," Damian said, pointing to the couple. "We call him Preach." They were young, probably in their late twenties or early thirties. He reminded Abby of her biology teacher from North Gwinnett. She liked him already.

"Welcome to the group, everybody," Pastor Doug said as he put his arm around his wife. "This is Shelly, the love of my life, though she's not here at the Bistro all that often. And this lady here"—he held out his hand—"Coach Mathews, needs no introduction. If you don't know her from Emerson, you will as soon as you start school. Some of this will be new to her, but we're so glad she'll be part of the Bistro team."

Shelly and Coach Mathews went back to their preparations.

"Thanks for the intros, Damian," Pastor Doug said. "We'll eat in just a minute, but I thought that before we jump into the getting-to-know-you introductions for the whole group, I'd read you a little passage." He put his arm around Damian, who was standing next to him. "By the way, I need to tell you that Damian loves the Lord, even though he talks fast and plays hard."

"It's true," Damian said. "But I'm learning. I want to be a good leader. We had a few complaints last year about being *inappropriate*." He used air quotes to set off the word inappropriate. "We've agreed to tone it down this year, but"—he paused and broke into a big grin—"we'll still do nicknames."

Several kids groaned.

"Hey, you guys, we're known here at the Bistro for our brilliant wit, snappy comebacks, and, most of all, our way-too-cool nicknames. Everybody eventually gets a nickname around here."

Abby looked around the room. There seemed to be a big difference between the kids sitting at the head table and the kids sitting at the bistro tables. She wasn't so sure Damian's description of brilliant and snappy extended much past the head table. Everyone else looked—well—nice and ordinary.

Pastor Doug opened his Bible. "Speaking of nicknames, I thought I'd read to you about names, since God seems to put a lot of stock in them. I'm reading from the sixty-second chapter of Isaiah, the second verse: 'The nations will see your righteousness, and all kings your glory; you will be called by a new name that the mouth of the LORD will bestow.'" He set the Bible down. "Damian and his crew love nicknaming. He assures me it is all in fun, but naming is important business. Think about how many times in the Bible God changed someone's name to reflect who he would become."

Shelly and Coach Mathews came up beside Pastor Doug, signaling that the food was ready.

"Anyway, it's time to ask the blessing and eat, but when we offer our names by way of introduction tonight, I wanted you to know how important it is."

After he prayed, Shelly gave instructions about picking up the pizza and drinks. Before Abby stood up to get in line, she introduced herself to the girl at her table. "Hi. I'm Abby. I'm new."

"I'm Ashley. I'm a freshman, so I'm new to the group too." She pointed to the head table. "Parker's my brother."

Abby almost said how cute she thought Parker was but stopped herself. How dumb would that be? She made her way with Ashley to the counter. She did like the way Parker looked, though. He had spiky hair with blond highlights and walked with a gait that only tall, lean guys had. She wondered if he played basketball. Best of all, though, was his smile.

Abby got her pizza and soft drink and walked back to the table with Ashley.

"Do you mind if I join you?" Parker asked, coming up behind them.

Abby wanted to sound welcoming, but it came out as "No, we don't mind—I mean, yes, join us." *Dumb.*

"It's older brothers who hate hanging around with little sisters," Ashley said. "Not the other way around. Yes, you can sit here."

He laughed as he turned toward Abby. "You're new, right?"

"Coach Mathews called and invited me."

"Will you be going to Emerson?" he asked.

"Yes," Abby answered.

"Me, too," Ashley said. "Parker's a senior, and I'll be a freshman."

The small talk continued. Abby figured it was just because the Bistro leadership team was probably supposed to mingle with the new people. But when she looked at the head table and saw all the Bistro Bs laughing together, she wondered.

"Aren't you supposed to be sitting with your team?" she asked.

"My team?" Parker seemed confused until he followed her eyes to Damian and the others. "Oh, you mean the Bistro team."

"Parker plays sports. He was probably thinking football team or basketball team," Ashley said.

"I think I can explain myself, little sister." He made like he was going to pull her pizza away until she swatted his hand. "Damian and the Bs are chatting away. I'm not really on their level conversation-wise."

Abby tilted her head. What did that mean?

He seemed to read her unspoken question. "I mean, they are sharp and quick—as Damian always says, they are wicked funny." Parker smiled that almost-shy smile. "I always get left in their dust."

"I've already heard about the nickname thing and am scared," Ashley said.

"Not everyone gets a nickname right away. It sort of takes time for one to grow unless something hits Damian immediately."

"I don't understand," Abby said. "My old youth group never did nicknames."

"Damian feels it sort of melds the group together."

"That's not what I hear," Ashley said, pulling a dangling string of cheese off her piece of pizza.

At the front table, Damian stood up. "Okay, kiddies, listen up."

Ashley leaned over to whisper to Abby, "You can tell he got through the food line first. He's done and ready to start while we all have our faces stuffed with pizza."

Abby laughed. Ashley might be a freshman, but she had attitude. Jen and Michelle would have loved her.

A wave of homesickness swept over Abby at the thought of Jen, Michelle, and her old youth group. She didn't want to prejudge the Bistro, but it already felt so different from her group at home.

"Again, welcome, everyone. Bank, will you open with prayer?"

The girl earlier introduced as Trina led a quick prayer.

"Park, we'll dispense with business today. You want to introduce your program?"

Parker walked up toward the front. When he got up there, he leaned against the head table in a relaxed stance. "We wanted this kickoff meeting to be a time to get to know each other, but we don't want to put any-one on the spot . . . "

"We don't?" Damian, sitting right behind him, did a sort of twist to an imaginary evil mustache, Simon Legree style.

"No. We don't." Parker smiled.

That smile. It was definitely an encouraging smile. Her old pastor would have guessed that Parker had the gift of encouragement just from that smile alone.

"We asked everyone to bring photos or souvenirs that show what you did this summer," he continued. "Coach Mathews and I figured it would be a good way to connect."

Andrea—the one Damian called Bistro Babe— raised her hand. Because she also sat behind Parker, she didn't wait for him to acknowledge her. "Excuse me, but I thought we stopped doing 'what I did on my summer vacation' essays in third grade."

Coach Mathews looked surprised by the criticism.

"Good one, Babe," Damian said, licking his finger and drawing a hash mark in the air.

Andrea grinned.

"To those who are new"—Parker gave an audible sigh—"that is a taste of what Damian calls 'witty repartee.' My advice is to just ignore it."

"Whoa! Dissed by Parker? That's a new one." Damian licked his finger again and sketched the point in the air. "I hate to do it, but I'll have to give this point to Park."

Abby watched this interchange. So far it seemed like a Damian and the Bistro Bs show. The people at the tables had barely moved. She caught a perplexed look on Coach Mathews' face. So she didn't get it either. Pastor Doug and Shelly were still working in the kitchen, straightening things up.

"If we can suspend the wit wars for a moment," Coach Mathews said, "we can get on with the intros."

"Touché," Damian said, but Coach didn't respond.

"We don't want to put anyone on the spot, so I'll go first." Parker pulled a string from his pocket. "I spent a lot of time doing sports stuff this summer, getting ready for football and going to basketball camp, but the thing that meant the most to me were the Wednesdays I worked at St. Anthony's."

St. Anthony's? Abby didn't know what that was. Parker must have seen the question on her face.

"For those of you who don't know, St. Anthony's is

the soup kitchen over on Jones Street in the Tenderloin. They feed more than two thousand homeless and poor people every day. I helped serve food."

"So how does the string tie in?" Coach Mathews asked.

"One day, as a thank-you, an old woman opened her bag and gave me this as a gift. She told me how she saw some kids in the city wearing a string tied around their wrists. She wanted to give me something." Parker stopped for a minute. "It means so much to me. If you knew how little . . . "

Abby could tell that he was uncomfortable sharing so much.

"Anyway, I'm going to wear my bracelet proudly, and I'm going to keep working at St. Anthony's throughout the year. They did far more for me than I did for them."

"Hear, hear," Damian said.

"Okay. I went first. I'd love to have someone new introduce themselves and tell us their summer story." Parker waited. No one volunteered. "Ashley? Would you be willing?"

As she walked to the front of the Bistro, Ashley gave him a look that promised payback would come later.

"Hi. I'm Ashley, Parker's sister." She turned and gave her brother an air punch. "You can see my brother picks on me . . . "

"Stop the presses." Damian stood up. "We have our first nickname." He made a theatrical gesture toward Ashley. "From now on you shall be known as . . . Sissy."

Ashley groaned. "Well, I hate being defined by relationship to my brother, but I know it could be worse."

Coach Mathews spoke up. "If we don't move along, we will only get to know a handful of people."

"Okay," Ashley said. "I brought my brand-new Emerson student-body card as my show-and-tell, because I spent much of my summer obsessing about having to start high school. I'll be a freshman, and I'm still a nervous wreck."

Parker smiled. "Thanks, *Sissy*." He emphasized the nickname. "How about introducing us to the newcomer at your table?"

Abby's mouth went dry. With all the banter, she was sure they'd never get around to her. How could she get up and walk down there and stand in front of all these people?

"This is Abby." Ashley headed back toward their table. "Abby, come up and tell the rest, since I don't know much more than that."

Abby stood up and pulled at her sweater. *Why did I wear this?* As she moved between the tables, she felt herself brushing people as she went. *Why did I let myself get so fat? I'm the fattest person in this room.*

Parker motioned for her to stand where Ashley had stood.

"Hi. I'm Abby. Actually, Abigail Ann Lewis." She smiled and tried to tug on her jeans without anyone seeing. They were a little tight and tended to ride up. Everyone was looking at her. She wondered what they were thinking. No. She could guess.

"Here's my picture. I guess I'll pass it around. It's a shot of my mom and me closing the door on the moving van that would take us from Georgia to California."

Come on, Abby. At least try to be funny.

"Um, you may have noticed I have a little accent . . ." She put on her best Atlanta socialite accent. "Well, bless your hearts, I'm fixin' to tell y'all a secret." She lowered her voice. "I really talk normal. It's y'all who have a funny accent."

Parker laughed out loud. "So what have you done since you got here?"

"Eat." Abby couldn't believe she said it. Oh, well, better get it right out front and laugh at herself before others laughed at her.

"Oh, she's quick," Damian said, nodding his head. "I think I feel another nickname coming on."

"Please don't make it Georgia Peach or something else like that," Abby said.

"Never. That's too cliché. I'm thinking rhyme here. And since you already poked fun at your weight, we know you're a good sport."

Uh-oh.

"I can't decide between Ab the Slab or the Flabster."

"Damian!" Coach Mathews rose out of her chair.

"That's okay," Abby hurried to say. *Might as well look it in the face, right?* "As a nickname, Flabster certainly carries weight."

"Score." Damian raised his hands and clapped at Abby. "Then Flabster it is."

As Abby bumped her way to her seat, she thought about what Pastor Doug had said earlier about names. He was right. They definitely had power. She felt twice as fat going back to her seat as she had going up.

As others reluctantly came up to share, she was glad for their sake that Damian had run out of nickname inspiration for tonight.

Was this what it took to make new friends? She would've felt even worse if she hadn't kept catching Parker smiling at her. What was that about?

RealTV

Emerson High

3

Abby woke to a blanket of fog on her first day of school. Not that fog was all that unusual. The famous San Francisco cloud cover greeted them almost every morning.

She'd worried about what to wear for days. She didn't want to wear something that screamed "new school clothes," but none of her Georgia clothes fit. What did San Francisco kids wear to school? She'd watched kids around the city, and it looked as if they had the same basic kinds of looks she was used to—from normal to trendy to skater to Goth and all points in between—but each style seemed cranked up a notch or two from Georgia styles. If the look was preppy, it was even more polished. If a student wore anti-establishment gear, it reeked with attitude.

Back home her own style always stayed smack in the middle—jeans and a great top and maybe something quirky or fun like a bright handbag or a collection of bracelets. Here in San Francisco, though, she decided to dress subtly—to avoid notice. She was only too aware of her size. When she held up the jeans she planned to wear that morning, they looked enormous. How in the world did she manage to tip the scale at 173 pounds? It's not that she had ever been slender. When she left Suwanee she weighed a little over 145 pounds, but Jen had always said she'd carried it well. How did someone manage to put on more than 25 pounds in a handful of months?

✳   ✳   ✳

Enough worry about clothes and weight. It's too late for that now. She took a deep breath and entered the doors of her new school. Could any school in America be more different from North Gwinnett High? Abby couldn't believe the contrast between schools. The kids at Emerson seemed so sophisticated, so multicultural, so, well . . . different. *Stop it. Atlanta is as with-it as any inner city. It's not like I'm coming from a rural one-room school.*

"Abby." Parker came up alongside her. "Hey, do I get to be first to welcome you to Emerson?"

"As a matter of fact, yes." Abby stopped, moving out of the traffic stream. "You have no idea how nice it is to be welcomed. I was feeling like a fish out of water—flopping around, gasping for air." She tried for a light tone.

"Surely not that bad."

"Well, close."

"Isabella." Parker turned and called out to a slender girl headed toward them. He turned toward Abby. "Stay here. This is someone I want you to meet."

The girl had straight brown hair tied back in a ponytail, and was slightly freckled. She seemed friendly, like someone Abby would want to get to know.

"Abby," Parker said, dragging Isabella over, "this is Isabella. She's way smart and way fun."

"Some intro, Parker," Isabella said with a smile as she slid her backpack off and set it on the floor.

"This is Abby," Parker said, ignoring the jab. "She's new to Emerson. Actually, she's new to San Francisco."

"From?" Isabella asked.

"Hi." Abby put out her hand. "I moved from Suwanee, a city near Atlanta."

"If you had spoken first, I might have guessed. My uncle lives in Atlanta, and we've visited, so the accent sounds familiar."

Abby smiled. "What accent?" she said, drawing out the last syllable.

Isabella laughed.

"See? I knew you'd like her," Parker said.

Abby smiled at Parker. What a nice thing to say.

Just then Damian, Andrea, and Trina rounded the corner.

"Hey, kiddies," Damian said. "Wow, Park, you already hooked up with the Flabster on your first day? We need to put you permanently on the welcome wagon."

Abby cringed at the nickname. Why did he have to talk in that look-at-me volume?

"Damian!" Isabella said, turning around to face him full-on. "What an awful nickname."

"Isabella. Isabella. You're just jealous that I haven't come up with a nickname for you yet." Damian turned toward Abby. "We're friends, right?" He didn't wait for an answer. "She chose Flabster. Besides, Flabigail didn't seem quite right." He laughed at his own wittiness.

"We're going to be late, Boss," Trina said, grabbing Damian's arm. "Have a fun first day," she said over her shoulder to Abby.

Andrea trailed after them. "Hey, Park. Call me. I've got an idea for a program for the Bistro."

"Sure," Parker said. "I'll try and catch up with you at some point."

"The Bistro. Right." Isabella clipped the words off.

Abby wondered about the cynicism she detected in Isabella's voice. "You don't like the Bistro?"

"She's never come," Parker said, "though I keep asking . . . "

How could anyone turn Parker down?

There was something about him that Abby really liked. Maybe it was something as simple as niceness. Not to say he wasn't cool—he was, but he didn't seem to be aware of it. No, he was nice. He said what he meant, he listened when someone else talked, and he seemed interested and engaged in life.

"And she keeps saying she'll come, but . . . " Parker looked to Abby.

"I went last week," Abby said, hoping she hadn't missed too much of what they had been saying.

"Is that where you got that nickname?" Isabella

asked. "I get so tired of the put-downs. That's why I haven't come, Parker."

"I know." Parker shifted his weight onto his other leg. "Damian thinks it makes people feel part of the group, almost like a secret handshake or something."

Isabella turned to Abby. "Is that how you felt when Damian gave you that nickname? Did you feel like you were in . . . part of the inner circle?"

Just then the warning bell rang. Abby laughed. "Saved by the bell. I need to go to the office to check in and pick up my schedule."

"Want me to come?" Parker asked.

"No. When we came to register I walked around the school, so I wouldn't look like a lost soul today. I think I can find everything."

"If you get fifth-period lunch, want to sit together?" Isabella asked. "My friend Celia's dad was transferred to Boston over the summer, and I'm currently best-friend-less. I spent the summer visualizing myself eating alone every day."

Abby couldn't believe this. She, too, figured she'd be one of those solitary diners. By the time you reached upperclassman status, everyone had solid friendships, and it was nearly impossible to break in.

"You can join us, Parker, if you quit twisting my arm to come to your church." Isabella smiled.

Parker laughed. "I'm not sure I can promise anything, but if you don't let me sit with you and Abby, I may just have to hover around your table, passing out religious tracts or something."

Isabella laughed. "Abby, you have to save me from this zealot. Try to get fifth-period lunch."

"I'll do my best. Save me a seat." She started to go

but turned around. "Save one for Parker too. He introduced me to you, so I'm thinking I owe him."

Parker gave her the thumbs-up.

Abby couldn't stop smiling as she headed to the office. She liked Parker, and she liked Isabella. Not bad for the first day of school.

✳   ✳   ✳

"Okay. I think I must be in California," Abby said as she slid in next to Isabella. "My friends in Suwanee will never believe the cafeteria has a full-service salad bar."

"Salad is healthy," Isabella said between bites. "What did you have in Georgia?"

"Regular cafeteria food—hamburgers, hot dogs, fries, tacos . . . you know."

Isabella made a face. "I'd be a blimp if I ate that stuff."

Abby didn't know what to say.

Isabella stopped midbite. "I can't believe I just said that." She put her fork down. "You must be struggling with weight issues, right?"

"Whatever gave you that idea?" Abby said. She never used to be sarcastic. Where did that come from?

Isabella didn't react to the sting. "I think I saw you cringe when Damian called you that name."

"You mean Flabster?"

"I hate that kind of nickname." Isabella chased a cherry tomato around her plate with her fork, finally spearing it. "The worst put-down in my opinion is the kind that sums you up in one superficial description— like 'four eyes.'" She popped the tomato into her mouth and bit down. "Damian seems to have a knack for honing in on the most sensitive aspect of a person for his nicknames."

"I don't think he means to hurt," Abby said, opening her bag of potato chips.

"Probably not on the surface. And who knows what lurks underneath." Isabella took a cucumber slice and dipped it in ranch dressing. "But it's a put-down all the same."

"I don't know . . ."

"How do you feel about your body?"

"What a weird thing to ask." Abby didn't like the turn of this conversation. *Does Isabella think she's some kind of shrink?*

Isabella laughed. "I forgot. You don't know me yet. My family is made up of a bunch of health nuts. My brother's a runner . . . a good runner. He's over at Cal. My dad's a cardiologist, and my mom's a nutritionist. They both work at UC Med Center."

Parker put his tray on the table next to Abby. "Don't even start with me, Isabella." He held up a brownie. "I know—evil incarnate."

"Well, there are better ways to consume that many calories." She put a finger on her cheek as if to calculate. "Let's see, carbs, fat—"

"Don't forget the magical ingredient, chocolate," Parker said.

"Right. Caffeine."

Parker turned to Abby. "Can you believe she accuses me of being a zealot?"

"Oh, leave me alone," Isabella said, laughing as she took another bite of salad. "It's in my blood."

"Blood that freely flows through cholesterol-free veins, right?" Parker said.

"You're just jealous." Isabella pretended to ignore Parker. "Back to our discussion, Abby—"

"That's okay," Abby said, cutting her off. She did not want to discuss her weight problems in front of Parker.

"So what were you two discussing?"

"We were talking about Damian's nicknames," Abby said. It was true. They had been before Isabella focused on Abby's weight.

"Did he hurt your feelings with your nickname, Abby?" Parker asked.

Before Abby could answer, Isabella spoke. "What do you think, Parker?"

"I don't know. I guess Abby seems so self-confident . . . "

"Self-confident?" That blew Abby away. *Me? Self-confident?*

"Aren't you?" Parker asked.

It seemed like he really wanted to know. Abby thought about what her dad used to say about actively making friends. One of the ways you deepened friendship was to share deeper stuff. She liked both Parker and Isabella. Could she trust them?

She looked at Isabella. Here was someone she'd like to know more, someone who seemed open to friendship. And Parker . . . well, she knew she liked what she saw so far.

"You have no idea how wobbly my confidence is at this point," she said. "And not because of the nickname."

Isabella put her fork down to listen.

"My dad died on February second—something with his aorta. One day he was alive, and I was in the middle of my life in Suwanee, and the next day that life was over."

Parker made a sound like a soft groan.

"It was so hard to be in Suwanee—to sit in church and have an empty place where Dad used to sit, to have his half of the garage empty, to have . . . well, you get the picture."

"Oh, Abby." Isabella's eyes got red. "I can't even imagine what that would be like. My dad's gone a lot, but . . . "

"Yeah, well . . . " Abby didn't want sympathy. It was too hard to hold things together when people were too sympathetic. "Mom and I decided to take a break from it all and come to San Francisco."

"Why San Fran?" Parker asked.

"Mom grew up here, and we could move in with her mother for a while."

"Where do you live?" Isabella asked. "I don't think you told me."

"On Eleventh Avenue almost at Lincoln."

Parker whistled. "Not too shabby. Cross Lincoln and you're in the park."

Anyone who knew San Francisco knew that property around Golden Gate Park was prime real estate, but to Abby it was a safe haven. It was Cece's home. Back when her grandparents first moved there it was just a nice neighborhood with lovely old homes.

Isabella still seemed shaken. "It must be so hard. To lose your dad and then lose your home and your friends."

"It is." There was no sense in denying it. "Mom and I keep talking about it as if it's an adventure, but . . . "

"So when did you get here?" Parker asked.

"We moved as soon as school was out." Abby took a breath. "In fact, that's why I started this story. Isabella and I were talking about weight, and then you asked me about self-confidence." Abby put her bag of chips down. "I must be an emotional eater. Ever since we got here, I've been living in my cocoon—reading, watching TV, and eating."

"You probably needed it," Isabella said.

"Maybe so, but when it came time to get out and re-join the world, instead of a butterfly emerging from the cocoon, a slug crawled out."

"Oh, Abby, please don't be self-deprecating. Do you have any idea how beautiful you are?" Isabella put her hand over Abby's on the table.

"I was not saying that to fish for a compliment," Abby said.

"I know. But I mean it."

Parker stood up. "Let me take your trays. I'm going to get another milk."

After he left, Isabella continued. "Don't underestimate yourself, Abby. I love your blonde hair with your brown eyes. How many people have that combination?"

"Thanks, but it's my weight that's my problem." She leaned in to Isabella. "I'm 173 pounds. How does a girl gain that much in one summer?"

"My mom would say that's not unusual in the teen years, especially during an emotional upheaval."

"Maybe I need to meet your mom." Abby laughed. "I've been feeling like the Poppin' Fresh dough boy, sabotaged with way too much yeast."

Isabella laughed. "See? That's why I knew I'd like you as soon as Parker introduced us. It's that smile."

"I guess we're going to owe Parker," Abby said. She'd practically bared her soul to Isabella, and it hadn't scared her away. *Thank You, God. I never expected to find a*

friend my first day of school. Help me be the friend Isabella
needs as well.

"You owe me for what?" Parker said as he sat back down.

"Be careful around this guy," Isabella said. "His ears are tuned to catch his name in any conversation."

Parker snorted.

"I've got PE next with Coach Mathews," Abby said, looking at her schedule.

"Me too," Isabella said. "You'll love her."

"I already met her at the Bistro."

"See," Parker said, "you need to come, Isabella. Abby, Coach Mathews . . . what's not to like?"

"Yo! Park, Flabster, Isabella." Damian and the Bs stopped by the table on their way out the door.

Isabella ignored him and turned back to Parker. "Let's see . . . what's not to like?"

4

"Far too many schools are doing away with physical education," Coach Mathews said as she passed out what she had called the "journals." Thirty-some girls sat with Abby and Isabella on bleachers in the gym. Luckily, they wore regular clothes. Isabella said they probably wouldn't have to dress till next week.

Abby dreaded that part of PE. Last time she showered at school she had been more than twenty pounds lighter. Most girls worried about sweat and showers ruining their hair and makeup. For Abby, those were the least of her worries. She looked around to see if she was the most overweight. No. There were at least two others who looked equally uncomfortable.

Stop that. She couldn't believe she'd just been relieved to see a couple of other girls with weight problems. This comparison stuff reeked. *What's happening to me?*

Coach handed each student a spiral-bound book. "Don't thumb through the journal just yet. We'll be going over these page by page during this introductory week."

Abby had been surprised to find physical education on her schedule. She'd finished the minimum PE requirement in Georgia, but since she figured that being in a class with Isabella might be fun, she decided not to request a change in her schedule. And so far, she liked what she had seen of Coach Mathews.

"I plan to take a holistic approach to phys ed," Coach said. "Who can give me the definition of *holistic?*"

A girl in the back said, "Isn't it kind of a religious, Zen-type of thing?"

"No, stupid," said another girl sitting next to the first one. "*Holistic* comes from the word *whole.*"

"You're right, McKinney, but let me stop you right there." Coach Mathews took her glasses off and looked directly at her. "I believe you just called Jamison 'stupid.'"

Everyone turned around to look at the two girls. They both seemed surprised.

"That is the last time—the very last time—anyone will use a derogatory name in my class without stiff consequences," Coach Mathews said.

"But I call her stupid all the time," the girl called McKinney said. "She's my friend. She doesn't mind."

"I have trouble believing she doesn't mind," Coach Mathews said. "But even if that were true, *I* mind."

McKinney made an exasperated sound.

Coach ignored her and let her eyes scan the whole class. "Words are powerful weapons that we treat too casually. They wound, and, believe me, those wounds can fester for years. Think back to the Columbine tragedy and the ones that followed." She set her sheaf of papers on the bleachers. "I often wonder how many cruel words it took to finally make one of those kids feel like an outsider."

The bleachers creaked as several girls shifted in their seats. Abby knew that no one wanted a lecture on her first day, but Coach Mathews had a point. They'd all seen their share of put-downs.

"I didn't mean to get off on a tangent, but remember —any cruel word spoken in this class will result in consequences. I expect you to guard your words."

"But what about during a game?" a girl in the front asked. "Like if someone misses an easy ball, for instance. We can't say anything?"

Coach Mathews didn't answer. She simply stood there, arms crossed.

"Oh, Coach. That's unnatural," the girl argued. "Yelling at your teammates helps keep everyone motivated."

"You could be right. It might be the norm, but we're going to try a new way. Even if you disagree, give it a shot. After all"—she picked up a red spiral-bound book and smiled—"I control the grade book, and good sportsmanship counts."

Abby liked her sense of humor. She wondered if Damian's nicknames the other night had anything to do with Coach Mathews' new policy. It would be interesting to see what happened next time they met at the Bistro.

"See? What did I say about mean words?" Isabella whispered to Abby. "Coach agrees with me."

"You two are definitely on the same wavelength," Abby whispered.

"Okay, back to the discussion," Coach Mathews said. "*Holistic* means a whole approach—an approach that covers many aspects and winds it into one." She picked up her copy of the journal. "I call it an integrated program. I want this body-conditioning class to be the first step in a lifelong health challenge."

Isabella grinned and poked Abby.

Abby already knew enough about her friend to know that Isabella would eat this up. As she said, it was in her blood.

"We're going to incorporate nutrition, sports, and exercise into this class."

Abby could see one group of girls down to the right whispering behind cupped hands. Several girls must have anticipated this class as a sort of free period.

"And you'll have homework."

This time the groans were audible.

"Oh, stop," Coach said, laughing. "If it were easy, you'd just take the class to escape an academic class."

Isabella whispered, "She's a mind reader. That's the reason this class is packed—they all wanted something easy."

"Okay, homework . . . " She thumbed through the pile of papers on the bench, choosing a binder. She opened the notebook. "First, I want each one of you to schedule a ten-minute consultation with me after school. We'll weigh you and take measurements so you have a starting place."

A girl sitting near Isabella raised her hand. "Do we have to? I mean, what if we don't want to be weighed? Isn't it a privacy thing?"

Coach Mathews didn't flinch. "Yes, you have to. It's a requirement of my course. If you have privacy issues, then you'll have to go to the office and change your schedule."

Abby opened her assignment book and wrote, "Make appointment with Coach." Had this class turned out to be more than she bargained for? The thought of stepping on the scale in front of anyone made her cringe.

"I'm also assigning you an ongoing task." Coach once again ignored their reactions. "I want you to watch the television show *Less is More* every Thursday night. I'll be giving a short quiz each Friday to make sure you watched."

"Cool," Isabella said. "I love that show."

Coach Mathews opened the journal. "Okay, let's take this page by page."

During the rest of the class they went over rules and looked at the weight charts, nutrition worksheets, and exercise graphs. By the time the bell rang, Abby figured there would be a mass exodus to the counseling office to try to change classes. As the girls filed out of the gym, they complained loudly. Apparently, no one had anticipated such an ambitious class.

"I'm going to like this class," Isabella said. "Where do you go next?"

"English."

"Okay, I'm off to the science building. What if we

57

plan to get together Thursday night to watch *Less is More?* I want you to meet my mom."

"Sounds good. I need to find out where you live, but I'll see you tomorrow at lunch, if not before."

✳   ✳   ✳

The week went quickly. On Thursday night Abby's mom dropped her off at Isabella's house over in Parkside, stopping briefly to meet Isabella's mom before taking her leave to get groceries for Cece. She said she'd stop by in an hour or so to pick Abby up.

Abby liked Isabella's house. It was a typical San Francisco house—newer than Cece's—maybe from the twenties or thirties. It still had the tall ceilings and bay windows on the front, and it still butted up next to the neighboring houses. Stand-alone houses were a rarity in San Francisco.

Isabella's furniture seemed newer, cushier, more modern, maybe; but they still had polished wooden floors and Oriental carpets like Cece's.

"Do you two have any kind of paper you need to fill out as you watch?" Isabella's mom asked as she led Abby into the room they called the library. She opened the doors on a built-in cabinet to reveal a huge flat-screen television.

"No." Isabella took the remote and switched on the TV. "But we'll have a quiz tomorrow."

Her mom left, and Isabella plumped up some cushions and pillows. "You can sit here on the couch or in that chair. Unless you'd rather pull up floor like I usually do."

Abby picked the chair. Isabella's mom came into the room with a tray.

"Are you going to watch with us, Dr. Kazan?" Abby asked.

"No. These are still reruns. They're only just auditioning people now for the next series that debuts in January." She set the plate of orange quarters and apple slices on the coffee table. "And please call me Carol. Dr. Kazan sounds like my work name."

"It also sounds like Dad's work name," Isabella said.

"That must get confusing." Abby picked up an apple slice. She could tell the Kazans were into health. No chips, no pretzels, no chocolate—no normal teen food for TV watching.

"I wonder how someone gets picked for the show," Isabella said.

"This show works with referrals," her mom said. "The reason I know the schedule and rerun status is that I get all the e-mail updates on the show. They are always looking for interesting contestants."

"Have you ever referred anyone?" Abby asked.

"Not yet. The person would have to fit a number of criteria. So far, none of my clients seem right." Isabella's mom put a bowl of raw almonds on the table.

"So, what criteria?" Isabella asked.

"Well, they want an overweight person but one whose weight does not exceed what can be safely lost in twelve two-week segments. They want someone with what they call a 'compelling human interest story.' And they want someone who lives in proximity to an available nutritionist and weight coach."

"Hmmm." Isabella took a slice of orange but seemed distracted.

"Oh, here it comes," Abby said. "Do you think we need to take notes?"

"I don't think so. I'll bet it's just general stuff to show we really watched."

They settled into the furniture to watch the opening credits, which included a short intro on each of the contestants.

"I wonder why they picked Gloria," Isabella said after watching her backstory. "When I watched this last season I got so tired of her complaining about the exercise and cheating on the food plan."

"Maybe she really intended to keep with the plan but found out how hard it is to stick with something when you're under stress."

"Is it?" Isabella muted the television for the first round of commercials. "When I'm under stress I use exercise and regular routine to keep things even in my life."

Weird. Abby never thought of exercise and stringent eating as a stress reducer. "I guess that proves we see food and exercise differently. I treat myself to comfort food, hot chocolate, and naps when I'm feeling bad."

"Mmmm. That sounds yummy—I mean, the hot chocolate part. Does it make you feel better?"

"I think so." Abby thought about it. "Well, temporarily, at least. After I get on the scale, it causes megastress."

Isabella turned the sound back on, and they settled in to watch. Today's episode began like all the others with the starting weigh-in. It was actually the ending weigh-in from the week before, replayed. The participants' success varied from a three-and-a-half-pound weight loss by one of the guys to a quarter-pound weight gain for Gloria. After the weigh-in, the camera crews followed the participants through their days at home, at work, and as they worked out with their trainers and consulted with their food coaches.

"I'll bet my mother could be a food coach," Isabella said.

"After being around you this week, I'm guessing you could be a food coach yourself. You know so much about nutrition."

"Look. There's Gloria cooking for her family and licking every spoon. I'll bet she just consumed a hundred extra calories and doesn't even know it."

"Give her a break. She's mixing brownies. Is there a person in the world who could mix a batch of brownies and not lick the spoon?"

Isabella didn't say anything.

"Don't tell me you could do it." Before Abby finished saying it, she knew her friend could do that very thing.

"If you keep a pan of warm soapy water in the sink, just plunge the utensil into the water before you have a chance to even imagine licking."

Abby took a pillow from behind her and flung it toward her friend's head. "You have no blood in your veins, Isabella. You must be a droid or something." She ducked as the pillow came sailing back. "Plunge a wooden spoon of brownie batter into soapy water . . . sacrilege."

"Okay. It was just a suggestion. I was trying out being a food coach." Isabella laughed. "I guess I failed."

Abby laughed. "Maybe you need to start with easier stuff, like taking the skin off chicken. Leave the chocolate abstinence for the advanced dieter."

"Are you thinking of trying to go on a diet?" Isabella asked.

Abby stopped laughing. "I don't know. I've never been successful at dieting."

"How long have you had a weight problem?"

"Too long." Abby was glad they had both seen this episode the first time around. She remembered enough to be able to pass a quiz. Besides, she'd much rather talk to Isabella. "In Georgia, I carried an extra twenty pounds, though my friends said it didn't look bad. I tried to lose it many times, but it never stayed off. When I'd finish dieting, I was so famished I couldn't stop eating."

"Mom calls that cyclical weight gain. You usually gain all the weight back plus a little more."

Abby nodded. That had been her experience. "After Dad died, I needed the comfort of food more than ever." She paused. "Plus, I didn't really care what happened."

Isabella didn't say anything. She reached for Abby's hand and held it for a moment before taking a handful of almonds.

Abby shrugged her shoulders. "I don't mean to blame it on grief or anything . . . "

"I don't think you are blaming grief. I think you are seeing how food is more than something to give you energy."

"But I get so mad at myself for letting everything get out of control." Abby stood up and walked over toward the window. "I've put on more than twenty pounds since Dad died. It makes my weight problem twice as bad as it was before."

"This really bugs you, doesn't it?" Isabella turned so she could look at Abby.

"It makes me crazy. Everything in my life is out of control, even my own body."

"Look at you, pacing," Isabella said.

Abby laughed. "Can you tell I'm a little worked up about this?"

"Yeah, but did you notice something?"

"What?"

"When you became upset, your body wanted to move. Maybe your body knows the best way to get rid of tension—exercise."

"Not a nap?" Abby said as she sat back down.

"Nope. That was for your cocooning time. This is your new adventure. Remember?"

Abby thought about that. Maybe Isabella had hit on something.

"Oh, look." Isabella pointed toward the screen. "I had forgotten about that." One of the guys who'd experienced the greatest weight loss had been riding a bike down an incline when he lost control and skidded. "He's going to be way sore. I wonder how that will affect his physical conditioning." Isabella groaned as he got up and tried to brush embedded gravel out of his abrasions.

The program followed each one throughout his or her two-week segment, covering the highs and the lows. The last scene showed each weigh-in. Each participant lost weight this week, though Gloria only lost the quarter pound she'd gained the week before. The bike crash victim still lost the most weight.

"It's not fair," Isabella said. "Guys always lose the most weight because of their muscle mass."

"Huh?" Abby said. Isabella's knowledge amazed Abby. It must come from living with two doctors.

"Muscle requires more energy and uses more calories, so if you have more muscle than fat—like a man—you use more calories."

"You are like a walking health encyclopedia." Abby took another apple slice even though it had darkened a little.

"I can't help it. If you knew my parents . . ."

"My mom's going to be coming before too long, so I probably won't get to meet your dad, but I like your mom."

"She's cool." Isabella turned off the television after the closing scene. "I never know when my dad's coming home. He does surgery, and it can take hours. Then he stays while his patient is settled into CCU and until he's comfortable that they're out of the woods. Sometimes he just sleeps at the hospital."

"He must be a good doctor."

"He is."

Abby wondered if a good heart doctor could have saved her dad. "I wish my dad had known him."

Isabella nodded. "When I told my dad about your father and that he was young and it was an aorta thing, my dad said it was too sad. Like there was no way around it."

"Yeah." What could anyone say? Abby kept wishing she could turn back the clock. That it was all a bad dream and she'd wake up and tell her dad about this awful nightmare.

"So what do you think Coach Mathews is going to ask us about *Less is More?*" Isabella asked, changing the subject.

"I don't know. Do you think her body-conditioning regimen is going to somehow be patterned after it?"

"How could she? We don't have individual trainers and food coaches."

"Could she do it with one trainer?" Abby asked.

"Who knows? But if anyone could do it, it would be Coach Mathews."

"I know. I really like her." Abby thought about the gathering at the Bistro the next night. "You should come with me to the Bistro tomorrow. You'd like seeing Coach Mathews outside of school."

"Thank you, but I'll pass." Isabella made a face.

"Because of Damian?"

"I don't know if it's Damian himself or even his faithful trio, although they do get under my skin . . . "

"What is it, then?" Abby really wanted to know.

"I don't want to hurt your feelings. I mean, it is your church and everything."

"What?" Abby took her leg and draped it over the arm of the chair. The furniture in the library had a worn, comfortable feel that invited relaxing. "I'm new to the church and to the Bistro, but I'd enjoy it so much more if my best friend were there."

"Best friend," Isabella said, trying on the words for size. "Boy, does it feel good to realize I have a best friend again."

"I know. Me too. I'm so glad you were here. I'm not glad your friend Celia moved away, but it feels like a God-thing that you were alone."

"A God-thing? What do you mean?"

How do I explain a God-thing? "I believe God knew we both needed each other. He knew we'd meet—part of His plan."

"Whoa. You're losing me there." Isabella leaned back. "I kind of believe in God. I mean, there's too much coincidence for me if there is no God—creation and all—but . . . "

"But?" Abby could tell a big "but" was coming.

"Well, it just sort of blows me away that you could believe God has a plan for my life." Isabella shook her head. "Abby, I don't mean to bring up stuff, and if you'd rather not . . . "

"What? No, go ahead." Abby couldn't quite figure where Isabella was going, but she felt as if this was a good place to open things up with her friend. After all, Abby's relationship to the Lord loomed large in her life. She could have never made it through the last seven months without her faith.

She and Isabella had not yet talked about spiritual things, but she knew from Parker that he'd been trying to get her to come to the Bistro or church, but so far, she'd resisted.

Isabella dug her toes into the couch, pulled her knees up to her chest, and wrapped her arms around them. "How can you talk about God being in control of something like bringing us together when He let your father die?"

Abby didn't say anything. How she'd struggled with this herself. Mom said it was the age-old question: How does a loving God let bad things happen to good people?

Isabella broke the silence. "I'm sorry, Abby. I never should have said that. I didn't mean to hurt you."

"No. You didn't hurt me," Abby said. "I just didn't know how to explain it."

"It sounds so harsh when I put it in words, though."

"I know, but I understand what you're asking." She ran her hands through her hair. "Believe me, I've questioned the same thing." *How to phrase it . . .* "The only thing I can say is that ever since I was little I've come to know Jesus a little better through the years. My dad loved Him too. I don't know why my dad died, and many times I tried to question God about it. I mean, couldn't He have taken somebody else if He needed someone?" Abby paused and laughed. "Okay, that's dumb, but you know how messed up our reasoning gets when reason gets tangled up with our heart."

"I know. It's hard to make sense of things when we're hurting." Isabella hugged her knees tighter.

"But here's what I do know. During my whole nightmare, God's been beside me. Sometimes I almost feel as if I could reach out and find His arm with my hand. I can't explain it . . . "

Isabella didn't say anything.

"Does it sound weird to say that I just know He's here and that He loves me and my mom and even my dad? In spite of Dad's death, I'm positive God's still in charge."

Isabella moved her head back and forth, as if calculating. "Are you sure this isn't part of the grief thing? Like you're in denial or something?"

"I don't know. You'd just have to get to know Him. It doesn't make sense, but once you get to know Him . . . "

"When you talk about God like that . . . like He's a person, it makes me want to sort of try it out."

"You'd love Him. I know it." Abby wished she knew how to share her faith better. She'd give anything to help Isabella reach out to Jesus.

"I don't doubt what you say. If you could go through what you are going through and still keep your faith, there must be something to it, but . . . "

"Another 'but,' huh?"

"I don't know. I do see something different in you. Like Parker. There definitely *is* something there, but most church people are no different at all."

"Most church people?"

"Okay, we're back to Damian and his group. When I see the put-downs and the way he . . . oh, I don't know." Isabella stood up and went to look out the window.

"I know what you're saying," Abby said. "But you can't judge the Lord by His followers. I mean, a lot of people think that church people should be good. The truth is, we know we're far from good, and we know better than anyone how much we need saving."

"Good point."

"My dad used to say that the church is not a museum for saints but a hospital for sinners."

Isabella looked distracted. "Shoot, your mom is here," Isabella said as she walked over to help Abby gather her things. "Hey, well, don't forget to save a place for me at lunch."

"Like I would forget. Hopefully, we watched enough of the show to pass this quiz. What do you think about going with me to the Bistro?"

Isabella rubbed her forehead. "How about if I come with you to church on Sunday instead?"

As Abby ran out to where her mom had double-parked, she worried about Isabella's feelings toward their youth group. She wished her friend could be part of her church life as well. At least she'd agreed to come on Sunday. What was it about the Bistro?

Postgame Bistro

5

"Yo, kiddies." Damian rapped on the table. "Settle down."

Many new faces filled the tables at the Bistro tonight since Coach and Pastor Doug pushed back the starting time until after the first home football game. Emerson won, so the mood was upbeat.

"We have lots of new people here, so let me introduce our Bistro team. You know me as Damian, but here, I'm the Bistro Boss. My right-hand man"—Damian raised an eyebrow and coughed—"excuse me, right-hand woman, is the Bistro Babe."

Andrea stood up and waved.

Damian held out his hand toward the other two girls. "To her left—your right—is, in order, Bistro Bunny and Bistro Bank."

Both girls stood together and waved.

"Bank, hold up your can." Damian walked over to Trina. "The Bistro is always free, but you're welcome to drop in a few coins or even a dollar or two to help pay for food." He jingled the can. "Or . . . if you happened to bet on tonight's game and picked the right team"— he paused for the fist waves and the round of "woo-woo-woo" roars—"drop in some of your winnings."

Abby looked at Coach standing near the kitchen. She looked none too happy. Emerson prohibited any kind of gambling.

"Welcome, everyone," Coach interrupted as she stepped forward to stand next to Damian.

He jumped slightly and turned to look at her with raised eyebrows but didn't say anything.

"Ignore Damian. He's kidding about gambling, of course. Not only does the school forbid betting, but this Book does as well." She moved to put her hand on Pastor Doug's Bible, sitting at the end of the table.

"I'm Coach Mathews. I think most of you know me. Standing over by the beverages is Pastor Doug."

Pastor Doug came up to stand by Coach. "Thanks, Coach. Thanks, Damian. We're excited about the win, and we're excited to see so many of you here. Be sure to mingle and meet each other. Let me open with a prayer, and later I'll close with a few words of meditation." He prayed, asking God to bless the food and the friendships.

Abby sat near Ashley again. "Where's Parker?" she asked.

Ashley looked around the room. "He'll probably be here soon. After the game his football coach usually talks to the team, and then they shower and stuff."

As if on cue, Parker came walking in. His hair was still damp but spiked. No question, he was what Michelle would have called a "hottie." He looked around the room until he saw Abby. Or was it his sister he saw?

"One of the conquering heroes," Damian called out. "This is Park, our program chairman."

Parker moved back toward the doorway before lifting his hand.

"Before we set up games, let me give you the rundown on eats." Damian looked over at Abby. "Flabster. Can you come and guide the food line?"

Abby hated to stand up. Flabster. Nothing like an announcement telling everyone to scope out her too-tight jeans and the arms that looked like fat sausages in a too-snug casing. *Why didn't I throw on that oversized sweatshirt?*

"Now don't go shy on us." Damian laughed, and several people laughed with him.

Abby's heart began to beat hard until she could hear the blood rushing in her ears. *Is this what it felt like when Dad had his heart thing?*

Coach Mathews stepped forward again. "Damian likes nicknames, but this is Abigail, everyone. She's new to San Francisco."

Abby stood up as her eyes met Parker's. He looked down. Was he embarrassed at the way she looked? *Maybe Damian is right; it's better to acknowledge weakness*

71

yourself—to laugh about it—than to let others laugh behind your back.

"Here I am." She waved. "I can't guess why the Boss calls me the Flabster." She put her hands on her way-too-ample hips. "Except that he says it's better than Flabigail."

Damian hooted and clapped. "She's a sport."

Coach Mathews crossed her arms across her chest but said nothing.

"Pay attention, kiddies," Damian said. "If you play nice, the Boss will find the perfect nickname for you too."

Abby made her way toward the food, and her heart slowed down some.

"Need help, Abby?" Parker asked.

"No."

He seemed disappointed. It didn't make sense. Abby stood by the food line as Damian gave instructions. The kids filed by, picking up chips and dips, brownies, and drinks.

As the food line dwindled, Coach Mathews leaned against the table by Abby. "I'm new to this group, but I'm sure having trouble with the nickname thing."

"Damian says it's like a secret handshake. It makes people feel like they belong," Abby said.

"Does your nickname make you feel like you belong?" She reached over to the veggie tray and took a piece of celery.

"I shouldn't let it bother me." Abby tried for a light tone, but the catch in her voice gave her away. "After all, it's true. Anyone can see that."

"I was talking with Isabella." Coach changed the subject. "I wanted her to join us here at the Bistro. She told me a little bit about your year."

Abby didn't know how she felt about that.

"She's excited about your new friendship."

"Me too. I wish we could get her to come here." Abby took a plate of chips and dip. "She did say she'd join me for church this Sunday."

"Good." Coach took a bottle of water. "She told me she's uncomfortable with what she thinks is a put-down atmosphere here at the Bistro."

"I know. I told her it definitely takes getting used to." Abby put a brownie on her plate.

"What do you think? Should we all get used to it, or should we try to change it?"

Abby considered that. "I don't know. I'm new, so I have no right to come into a group and try to change it, do I?"

"I'm new too, but I think the nicknaming is potentially dangerous." Coach took a long drink of water. "You seem pretty sure of yourself, so it may not bother you, but some of the kids are less confident."

That surprised Abby. *Me? Confident?* If only Coach knew the self-loathing that went on in her own mind. The nickname she'd been given was nothing compared to what she called herself. Each morning as she stood in front of the mirror, she found herself saying words like *slob, fatso, oinker.* Once she had finally rejoined the world after her summer of seclusion, she was disgusted with what she'd become.

"It doesn't seem to bother anyone else, does it?" Abby hardly noticed others in her own shame.

"I caught Parker's reaction, and I don't think he's comfortable."

Abby didn't say anything. Could that be why Parker looked down? Maybe it wasn't about the way she looked but about being uncomfortable with Damian's nickname. Abby's mood lightened at the possibility.

"I need to talk to Pastor Doug and Damian," Coach Mathews said. "You're right. We're new and need to proceed slowly."

Abby nodded. "I just hope I can get Isabella to come."

"Me too." Coach sat down at a nearby table, and Abby followed. "Did you see *Less is More* last night?"

Abby laughed, figuring she hadn't graded the quizzes yet. "Let's see . . . " She put her finger against the side of her mouth as if to think. "It was an assignment, you know. Are you trying to trap me?"

Coach just laughed. "I really like the premise of the show—especially the trainer and food coach. I think the mentor-type model is exciting . . . and the accountability."

"I know. It's so easy to let the pounds creep on, but it takes almost an act of Congress to make the commitment to get them off."

"I'm trying to figure out how I could incorporate that model in our body-conditioning class."

"It's hard without the one-on-one part." Abby took a bite of brownie. *Chocolate. Mmmm.* "And not putting anyone down, but some of the girls in our class are naturally slim, and they don't have a clue."

"I know. I've battled weight my whole life. Those skinny people who say, 'Just eat less' . . . Well, let's not go there."

Abby laughed. "I can't believe you ever had a weight problem."

"It's one of the reasons I went into physical education. I learned from experience how important exercise and food can be."

"Is this a closed meeting?" Parker set his plate of food on the table.

"Join us," said Coach. "We're talking school."

Abby shot her a look of gratitude. She appreciated that Coach didn't say they were talking about weight.

"Isabella's coming to church with me on Sunday," Abby said to Parker.

"Good going. I can't tell you how long I've tried to get her to come to the Bistro."

"Well, neither of us could manage to talk her into the Bistro," Coach said.

Just then hooting erupted over by the computer area. Damian moved over to the area. He whistled to get everyone's attention. "Listen up, kiddies."

It took a couple more shrill whistles until the room quieted.

Damian climbed up onto a chair and pointed to a freshman next to him. "Gerald, here, has earned himself a nickname." The boy shoved his hands deep into his pockets and raised his shoulders toward his ears. He shifted his weight from one foot to the other and bit his lip. He looked more like a student being called into the dean's office than someone being singled out for an honor.

"Gerald just beat the all-time Slam City single-game high score set by now-graduated Sean Joseph." Damian lifted his hands to signal for applause. The group followed the unspoken instruction and clapped wildly.

"The Bistro Boss confers on Gerald . . . Stand on this chair, Gerald . . . "

Abby could see Gerald's discomfort. A flush of red crept up his neck and began to stain his cheeks. He stumbled as he tried to step up on the chair.

Parker took a deep breath in through his nostrils, shaking his head slightly.

"From now on," Damian continued, "you'll be known as Geek-Meister. Geek for short."

Gerald mumbled something as the crowd began to chant, "Geek, Geek, Geek." He stepped down, and Damian led the whistling and chanting.

Coach put her bottle of water down. "I don't know . . . ," she said.

Abby watched Gerald as his friends hit him on the back. As soon as he could, he slipped into the restrooms. Maybe Coach was right. It was even harder on some kids than others. She wondered if he hadn't had to live with the Geek label before.

"That's why Isabella won't come," Parker said. "She's heard about the nicknames and hates them."

"I'm going to discuss this dynamic with Pastor Doug. I'm not sure it's healthy," Coach said.

"I've tried to bring it up in Bistro leadership," Parker said, "but I always get shot down."

Abby finished the last of her chips.

"Damian is a strong leader. He feels his style is perfect for our peers. He says it's fast-paced, a little sarcastic with just enough attitude to keep things moving," Parker said.

"That's how he sees it?" Coach put her fingers over her lips. "Hmmm."

"He loves heading this group. I mean, he's a natural showman." Parker gestured toward Damian, who was entertaining a whole circle of students near the computers. "It's hard to criticize when the kids seem to flock to the Bistro. And listen to the decibel level in the room—everyone's having a great time."

"I don't know," Coach Mathews said as she moved toward the kitchen.

"So how are you getting home?" Parker asked Abby.

"My mom's going to swing by at eleven."

"If you want to walk next week, Ashley and I can walk you home afterward."

Abby smiled. That sounded like fun. "It won't be too far out of your way?"

"No. Besides, we like to walk the city. When I first got my license I wanted to drive everywhere, but you know how bad parking can be. I ended up going back to foot power mostly. That and Muni."

"Yeah. I was taking driver training in Georgia, but . . . " Abby didn't know how to finish the statement. "Well, everything changed."

"I know. Isabella told me about your pulling back after your dad died."

Abby sighed. "You're the second person tonight who mentioned that Isabella shared stuff about me."

Parker laughed. "Now don't go getting paranoid. Isabella would never share confidences. You can trust her."

"I know. I sense that already."

"She's been my friend since before junior high," Parker said. "She's a bud . . . the best."

"Never anything more?" Abby couldn't believe she asked that.

Parker didn't answer right away. "You know she's not a believer, right?"

Abby understood. "Yes. We had a good discussion about spiritual things last night."

"You did?" Parker leaned in. "Tell me about it."

Abby told him the highlights—about Isabella's concern about a God who allows bad things to happen.

Parker whistled. "Nothing like hitting the hardest question of all."

"I think Isabella wants belief to come from the intellect. The funny thing is that it's a heart thing."

"Yep. Totally throws us intellectuals for a loop." Parker pulled his mouth down in what he thought was a brainy look.

Abby laughed. "Don't try to fool me. You're a jock through and through."

Just then Coach happened by. "Oh no. Now you're doing it, Abby."

Abby laughed again. "Caught me. No, I wasn't calling names. Just teasing this 'intellectual' friend of mine."

Parker just laughed. "Keep talking to Isabella. I'm praying for her. Have been for the longest time."

"I will. She's my first best friend I've ever had who's not a Christian," Abby said. "I won't be able to help myself."

The gathering began to break up. Abby, Parker, and Ashley helped Coach clean up before Abby went out to see if her mom was there.

"See you guys Sunday," Abby said.

"I'll save a place for you and Isabella," Parker said as he waved.

Abby couldn't help wondering whether it was she or Isabella he most wanted to see.

So what did you think of church?" Abby asked Isabella as they walked toward the street with Parker.

"You know, you guys, it's not the first time I've been to church," Isabella said.

Abby laughed. "I didn't mean it like that."

"I hope you don't feel as if Abby and I are ganging up on you," Parker said. "It's just that the spiritual things mean so much to us, it's hard not to share."

"No," Isabella said, "I understand. I like it that we're friends. Friends share things we feel passionate about. I probably make you guys crazy with my talk of health and nutrition."

Abby stopped, looking at Isabella with mock seriousness. "Well, now that you mention it . . . "

"You stop," Isabella said, laughing. "I haven't even half begun on you."

"So," Parker came back to the first question, "what did you think of church?"

"I liked it . . . lots of food for thought. Hearing your pastor examine that passage from the Bible, piece by piece, made me want to find my old Bible and do a little reading."

Abby smiled. *Yes!* She couldn't have hoped for a better reaction. "If you can't find it, I'm sure I have an extra Bible."

"It's funny," Isabella said. "I consider myself well-read . . . at least for your average high school student, but this morning I realized I've barely skimmed the Bible. Even if I don't believe it like you two do, it is considered the most important book in Western civilization. Up until now, it's almost like I've been afraid to scratch the surface."

"At least you recognize how powerful it is," Parker said.

"I'm not so sure about that, but if I'm going to be a card-carrying skeptic, I'd better know what I'm disbelieving, right?"

"That makes a lot of sense." Abby appreciated Isabella's honesty. And she knew God would honor her friend's openness. "Mom and Cece are probably already home. They asked me to invite both of you to dinner."

"Tonight?" Isabella asked.

"No. I mean lunch. Midday. In Georgia, we always called it Sunday dinner."

"Sure," Parker said. "Let me run inside the church again and tell my mom."

"It'll be fun to see where you live." Isabella pulled out her cell phone. "I need to make sure it's okay."

A few minutes later the three were walking down Lincoln alongside the park. Sundays were the busiest day of the week at Golden Gate Park—people walking dogs, couples lounging on the grass, children flying kites in the fall breeze.

"I can't believe your grandmother lives this close to the park," Isabella said. "I don't even want to think what it would cost to move into your neighborhood."

Leave it to Isabella to think in terms of real estate. Abby could tell she was an only child living with two professional parents. "They bought it way before the war. I think Grandpa once said it cost them under ten thousand dollars."

Abby loved the walk. In Suwanee they had to drive everywhere—in the suburbs nothing was close enough. Since starting school, Abby walked everywhere. On a day like today, when she walked with two friends, she appreciated Cece's neighborhood more than ever.

"One small warning . . . ," she said as they neared Eleventh Avenue.

"What? Don't tell me there are bodies buried in the basement." Parker crossed in front of them to walk on the outside of the street. Old-fashioned manners were not totally dead. Abby wondered if it was a San Francisco thing—kind of a nod to the grand old city.

"Yeah, right." Abby gave him a light punch. "No, it's about my grandmother's cooking . . ."

"It's bad?" Isabella asked.

"Is the cooking the cause of the bodies in the basement?" Parker laughed at his own lame joke.

Abby ignored him. "It tastes good, but it's a little unusual." Abby hated beating around the bush. "Cece loves to combine lots of hokey prepared foods into new kinds of fancy concoctions with peppy names."

Isabella started to laugh. "I have a great aunt who does the same thing. You should see my dad roll his eyes when she serves her meals. Dad says he can feel his arteries clogging as soon as he turns down her street."

"I don't know what's wrong with that," Parker said. "My favorite food is beanie weenies. You open up a big can of pork 'n' beans and cut up a few Louisiana Hot Links into it. Heat it up, and you have a great meal."

The girls stopped midsidewalk as he described his favorite meal. Neither said a word, but both broke out into laughter at almost the same moment.

"What?" Parker asked innocently. "It's good."

They couldn't stop laughing as they crossed Lincoln and walked up the steps to Abby's house.

"You seem to be having fun," Mom said as she opened the door.

"Mom, this is Parker, and this is Isabella." Abby caught her breath. "Parker and Isabella, this is my mom."

Her friends greeted her mom; then Abby took them into the kitchen to meet Cece.

"So, what are you cooking, Mrs. Grady?" Parker asked after introductions were made. "It smells wonderful."

Both girls started giggling again.

"I'm making Savory Bean Casserole," she said.

Parker moved in to inhale the scent.

When Cece saw his interest, she said, "It's so easy. You just take a large can of kidney beans, a large can of baked beans, and a can of butter beans. First you fry a half-dozen slices of bacon . . . get them crisp. Sauté chopped onions as you fry up the bacon. You add the canned beans to the pan, then add half a bottle of ketchup, a half cup of brown sugar, a tablespoon of Worcestershire sauce, and a cup of shredded cheddar cheese. You pour it into a casserole dish and bake it." Cece wiped her hands on her apron. "It's easy."

Isabella looked at the counter, littered with cans and boxes. "Wouldn't it be easier to just make the beans from scratch? Cheaper too."

"And miss all the fun of combining stuff?" Cece was serious. "I can do it in one-fourth the time."

Parker nodded. "Sounds efficient."

"Speaking of efficient, look at these biscuits I found." She held up a basket of fluffy golden brown biscuits. "They come frozen. All you have to do is open their ziplock bag, take out the number you need, put them in the oven, and zip the bag back up."

Isabella picked up the bag and turned it over to read the nutrition information. When her finger scanned the calorie count per serving, she didn't say a word, but her raised eyebrows gave her away.

"Why don't you help me get the food on the table?" Cece grabbed the butter and the milk.

Abby took pot holders and carried the hot casserole dish into the dining room. Mom got the bowl of creamed corn out of the microwave.

"Get the honey for the biscuits," called Cece from the dining room. "It's right there on the counter. And bring the chocolate syrup for the milk."

Parker came in carrying both, and they sat down to pray.

As they started to eat, Isabella's eyes were glued to the milk carton. Abby knew she must have been aghast at the nutrition information for whole milk.

"Now I know you kids will drink more milk if you put chocolate in it, so here's a squeeze bottle of chocolate syrup. Help yourself."

Parker did just that. As he started to eat, he stopped every few minutes to compliment Cece on the food. "Mmmm, this is so good."

Cece beamed.

Abby knew that from now on Cece would refer to him as "that nice young man." He'd won her heart with his honest compliments.

"Anyone want to take a walk through the park . . . maybe around Stow Lake to work off dinner?" Isabella suggested after the dishes were done and Mom and Cece had gone down to the garden.

"Sounds like fun," Parker said.

The three friends talked and walked, crossing the street and finding the path. Isabella set the pace, but after they walked for a few minutes Abby got quieter and quieter. She found she not only couldn't keep up, but she no longer had enough air to both talk and walk at the same time. Parker and Isabella slowed their steps several times to pace themselves to her. Abby knew her red cheeks came from more than exertion.

"You two go on ahead," she finally said, panting. "This Southern-belle saunter is going to frustrate you." She didn't say that she was too out of shape to keep up a brisk walk.

"No," Parker said. "This is not an endurance competition. We want to have fun together."

"Besides," Isabella said, "look at how beautiful the park is on this almost-autumn afternoon. We won't see many more days as perfect as today."

Abby felt terrible. "Really, I don't mind. I'm pretty much out of shape."

Parker stopped. "Let's sit here on a bench for a minute." He spread his knees and leaned his elbows on them, stretching his back. "Don't worry about being out of shape, Abby. It happens. The only reason I'm in good shape now is football. We toned up during the summer."

"And the reason I'm fit is because my parents eat, sleep, and breathe fitness." Isabella laughed. "Don't ask . . ."

Abby didn't say anything, because the only thing she could handle was trying to slow her breathing down. She sounded like an asthmatic in the middle of a severe attack. She appreciated her friends' willingness to slow down for her, but she hated it at the same time. *How could you let this happen to you?* She knew it didn't do any good to beat herself up, but she couldn't help herself. *You've ended up the fattest, most out-of-shape girl at Emerson. The biggest laugh is that your two best friends turn out to be a football hero and the fitness queen.*

Miserable. That's how she felt.

※　　　※　　　※

"Dear Dad," Abby typed the greeting into a blank e-mail to the old address. "You were right. I stepped out just like you said, and I have two wonderful friends. You'd really like Isabella, and both of us feel lucky we found each other. It seems so funny that we're becoming such good friends, and yet she'll never get to know you. It's making me realize I've begun the after-Dad part of my life." That sounded too sad to even think about. She stopped for a minute.

"Okay, enough of that," she continued. "Mom and Cece like her. Can you pray that she'll come to know Jesus?" She stopped again and shook her head. "That's weird, huh? LOL. I don't know if you can still pray or not since you are right there with Jesus. I'm not too up on my Bible here—not too sure how things work, but if you can ask Jesus . . . " She laughed and just kept on typing. "Okay, forget that. I'll ask Jesus.

"And about Parker . . . I don't know how I feel. I like him a lot. Maybe he's just a guy friend, but maybe it'll be more. Who knows? I think you'd like him too."

Just then she heard the chime of someone instant messaging her. The instant message box covered part of her e-mail to Dad. It was from BistroBoss1.

"Yo, Flabster. Bs and I r going to Strbks now. Wanna come?"

She IMed him back. "Y?"

"Fun, Bistro stuff."

She thought about it a minute. "CU there."

She finished off her e-mail to her father, pressed Send, and went down to make sure Mom was okay with her meeting the Bs at Starbucks.

After a brisk walk—her second of the day—she opened the door of Starbucks. The warm smell of coffee and chocolate greeted her. She spotted Damian and slid into an empty chair at his table. Trina and Andrea were up at the counter getting drinks. Jamie must not have come yet.

"Hi, Damian," she said. "What's up?"

"Yo, Flabster. We planned to have a meeting about Bistro and thought about you."

She quirked an eyebrow as if to ask why, but he ignored the implied question.

"Where are Parker, Pastor Doug, and Coach?" she asked.

"Oh, this isn't an official meeting, only informal. Here come Babe and Bank." He scooted his chair over to make sure they had enough room. Andrea slid a mocha frap over to him. "Thanks, Babe."

"We'll wait while you get something," Trina said.

After Abby got a Caramel Macchiato, she rejoined them, still wondering why she was here. Jamie had come while Abby ordered.

Damian and the three girls seemed so unified—so much a team. In fact, she felt guilty, but she had trouble telling the three girls apart. Not that they looked alike, but she'd met them at the same time, and they each had a real name and a nickname. That was hard enough to keep straight, and then they always seemed to agree with Damian. She couldn't think of a single thing she knew about any of the three.

"Do all of you live close?" Abby asked.

Damian raised his hand as if to brush away the question. "Sort of." He pulled his chair closer and leaned in. "Here's what I've been thinking."

Abby sat back. As usual, Damian took charge. She could see why she didn't really know the Bs. Damian never let them get a word in. She had no idea why he had invited her, but she would make sure she didn't become his fourth B. *Good thing,* she thought. *I'd probably be named the Bistro Blimp. Flabster is bad enough.*

". . . So I'm thinking we need to do better." He looked at Abby, waiting for her agreement.

"I'm sorry. I missed the first—"

Andrea jumped in. "The Boss said he felt the food situation at the Bistro needed attention."

"I can speak for myself, Babe," he said, cutting her off. "We want the Bistro to be *the* place to be. It should be so popular that the only problem would be trying to squeeze everyone in without getting in trouble with the fire marshal. We have the coolest place, the coolest kids; now we need the coolest eats."

"Who does the food now?" Abby asked.

"It's kind of hit-and-miss. Sometimes the parents kick in; other times Pastor Doug pulls stuff out of the church food stash."

"Where would the money come from?" Trina asked. "I don't think the church can give us a bigger budget. They just remodeled the basement into the Bistro last year."

"We need an admission charge," Damian said. "Look at how many people came last week. It's obvious we've become *the* place to come."

Abby didn't say anything. She guessed an admission charge might keep several kids out.

"What about those kids who don't have money?" Jamie asked.

"There are lots of things they can come to at church that are free." Damian leaned back. "The Bistro has evolved into an unusual ministry. Most Christian things are sort of everybody-welcome kind of places. You know, inclusive."

No one interrupted.

"I mean, who else tries to reach the popular kids, the intellectuals, the movers and shakers?"

Abby felt like an audience to a one-man performance.

"You know," he continued, "my dad's involved in city politics, and he always says to reach for your influencers, your money people, your well-connected people, and the rest will follow."

"What does Pastor Doug think about that?" Abby asked.

Damian took a drink, pulling deeply on the straw. "I don't know that we've really talked about the philosophy. He does believe in choosing a leadership team and letting them lead, though."

"I think he knows he has a strong leader in the Boss," Andrea said.

"What about Coach?" Abby hadn't known Coach Mathews long, but she could guess what Coach would think of that.

"She's still new to us. Honestly? She doesn't get it yet."

Abby didn't say anything, but she had an idea that Coach would not be so easily dismissed.

"So did you invite me for an extra opinion?"

Damian laughed. "You are so funny, Flabster. I like that cynical wit."

Trina and Jamie laughed too, but Andrea just crossed her arms over her chest and glared at Abby.

Uh-oh. Andrea didn't like what she saw as Damian giving me a compliment. Some compliment.

"No, we invited you to see if you'd be our Bistro Munchies Coordinator." Damian didn't even wait for her reaction. "We see the Bistro offering a different menu each Friday of the month. Let's say the first Friday we offer Guacamole Bacon Cheeseburgers with french fries. You could set up a barbecue station outside the back door and—"

"Oh, that sounds good," Jamie said.

Damian smiled. "We could do all kinds of interesting things. Picture a Fisherman's wharf–style cracked crab feed with San Francisco sourdough for another night."

"And you think I could head that up?" Abby asked. "It sounds like a restaurant."

"Well, Parker said your grandmother is some kind of gourmet cook—"

Abby started to laugh.

Damian gave her a sharp look but kept on going. "And because you just moved here and don't have many friends or interests yet, we thought you'd be able to devote the time to it."

The girls all nodded.

"And we're trying to match people's interests with jobs, and it's obvious you're into food."

So that was it. Give the job to the fat girl with no friends and a grandmother who cooks. She had to suppress a giggle at the characterization of her grandmother as a gourmet cook. Wait until she told Mom.

"Well?" Damian asked.

"I appreciate your thinking of me, but it's way beyond my abilities. I can't even boil water." Abby realized that didn't tell the whole story. She needed to be honest. "My family has just been through a huge upheaval that led to our moving here. I honestly don't think we could take on anything this big yet."

Damian seemed perturbed. "Yeah, well, we've all got our little issues . . . "

Little issues. Abby looked at Damian. Pastor Doug had said that Damian loved the Lord. Abby had to take his word for it, but it looked as if Damian needed some work in the area of mercy.

"If you need help with leading a devotion or something like that, I'll be happy to help."

"Yeah, okay." Damian's tone of voice told her he was not a happy camper.

Abby was glad she had paid for her own drink. She could tell that Damian and the Bs considered this a wasted meeting. Oh, well.

❋   ❋   ❋

During the next several Bistro gatherings, Damian pointedly ignored Abby. He never even looked her way, let alone singled her out. He no longer even called her Flabster. Abby figured he wasn't used to having people decline his requests. The food stayed casual. Apparently Damian hadn't managed to find anyone else willing to whip up five-star meals on a nonexistent budget either.

Despite the snubs from Damian, she continued to enjoy the Bistro. Pastor Doug gave some fascinating devotions, and many of the kids showed interest. Attendance stayed high, but she still couldn't interest Isabella in coming.

Abby's friendship with Isabella continued to grow. She thought it was too bad they couldn't have met during the summer, since school kept them way too busy. They managed to squeeze out time to be together in spite of their schedules—sometimes at Isabella's home and sometimes at Cece's.

Parker joined them when he could, but between

football, the Bistro, schoolwork, and occasional volunteering at St. Anthony's, he stayed busier than both of them. Abby still didn't know where to file the relationship—friend, church bud, or something more.

She found that she enjoyed school. She once thought she'd never get over the loss of North Gwinnett High, but Emerson had its advantages. For one, Coach Mathews. Coach expected a lot, but her enthusiasm and encouragement made PE one of Abby's favorite classes. Who'd have ever thought it?

"Abby," Coach called to her. "Are you daydreaming, or are you going to get your stats recorded?"

Ugh. Stats were the one reason she couldn't say she loved PE. Nothing made her feel like a failure as much as weighing in and taking measurements. Luckily, Coach herself did the weighing and measuring. If another student were privy to her failure . . . well, it didn't bear thinking about.

She went into Coach's office and stepped on the scale. Coach tapped the weights back and forth a bit. The big weight was over on the fourth notch—the one-hundred-fifty-pound marker. The smaller weight was finally tapped over to the twenty-three-pound increment. After all the walking around the city, after all the aerobics in class, she still weighed in at a solid one hundred seventy-three pounds.

"Tracy Mathews?" The voice came over the intercom. "Please come to the office for an important phone call."

Whew! Saved by the bell, so to speak, thought Abby. At least she wouldn't have to be measured.

"I'll be back," Coach told her. Then to the class she said, "Keep doing what you are doing. I need to run to the office."

Isabella put down her free weights to come over to Abby. "How'd you do?"

"Lousy." Abby really thought she'd show a loss this week. "I've upped my exercise, but I guess nothing trumps Cece's stick-to-your-ribs cooking."

"Bummer. You've been working hard to increase your exercise. I really hoped to see a breakthrough. I guess Mom is right. Nutrition holds the key."

The intercom buzzed again. It always started with static before the voice came through. "Abigail Lewis. Isabella Kazan. Please come to the office." The message repeated, but since all the girls were making a loud "*Oooo*" sound, it drowned the words out.

"Oooo, you're in trouble now," one girl said.

Abby and Isabella just ignored the class with their catcalls, but it did seem strange that the office first called Coach Mathews and then the two friends.

What could it be?

Chosen

7

When they entered the office, they could see Coach sitting with the principal. The person sitting at the attendance desk said, "Go right in," and gestured toward the office.

Abby looked at Isabella. She didn't seem worried. In fact, her smile spread across her face. She knew something.

"What's up? What do you know?" Abby asked.

"I don't know anything for sure, but it could be fun." Isabella pulled Abby's hand. "Come on."

As they opened the door, Abby saw the excitement written on Coach's face.

"Good." Coach pulled two chairs toward the desk and indicated that they were to sit down.

The principal pressed a button on the phone and leaned down to speak into it. "Have Ms. Tinsman's aide go to the girls' PE room and supervise the rest of the period. Coach Mathews is tied up."

She looked up and said, "Tracy, why don't you tell the girls about the phone call you just received."

Coach shook her head as if in disbelief. "I just received a call from the producer of *Less is More.*"

"The television show?" Abby asked.

"Can you believe it? They are choosing contestants for the new season and, well . . . " Coach faltered. "Abby, I submitted your name. I probably should have asked first, but it was such a long shot, I didn't think it was a possibility."

"Me?" Abby sat still. She didn't know how she felt about it.

"They picked you, Abby. I can hardly believe it." She laughed. "But it's true. You are going to be a contestant on the new season of the show."

"Me?" Abby knew she sounded like an idiot, but it just wouldn't sink in.

"I called your mom, and she's on her way down here. We'll go over the details then and see if she's okay with it." Coach turned to Abby. "More importantly, are you okay with it?"

"It's going to be such fun, Abby," Isabella said.

Abby looked at Isabella, suddenly wondering why Coach included her in this meeting. "Did you have something to do with this?"

Before she even had a chance to answer, Abby's mom opened the door and came in.

Coach got up and pulled another seat into their circle. After introductions, she said, "I'm guessing you don't have any idea why we've called you to the school, right?"

"From the look on Abby's face, I'm wondering if she's been struck by a two-by-four."

Everyone laughed, including Abby.

"Mom, I just found out I've been chosen to be a contestant on *Less is More*." Abby said the words so she could see how they felt coming out of her mouth. Maybe if she said it enough, she might come to believe it.

"How did that happen?" Mom asked.

"I may have overstepped my bounds, Mrs. Lewis," Coach said. "But as I've gotten to know Abby, I've seen her struggling over the weight issue."

Abby didn't say anything. Here she thought she was so good at hiding her concern behind laughter.

"Please call me Karen," Mom said. "We should have met at church by now and been on a first-name basis. Abby's told me about you and how much she loves your class and your involvement with the Bistro. Now I can see how well-tuned you are to your students."

"Well, not all of my students yet, but Abby and I clicked right away. Isabella as well."

Abby looked at her friend. "I'm guessing Coach had help with this, right?"

Isabella laughed. "What gave you that idea?"

"Could it have been that your mom has been on the *Less is More* database? Could it be that I've seen a look on your face that told me you were cooking up some sort of idea more than once?" Abby gave her friend a couple of well-aimed pokes. "If I didn't like you so much . . . "

The principal said, "Part of the reason the producer chose Abby was because of the unique team approach Tracy proposed."

"Team approach?" Abby wondered if there would be more than one contestant.

"I'm crazy about the show, and so is Isabella. When we cooked up this plan, we decided that one of our distinctions could be that your personal trainer could be your good old phys ed instructor, and your food coach could be your best friend." Coach smiled. "They loved it."

"I think they plan to have some fun with the contrast of our home-grown team against teams with high-priced trainers and nutritionists," the principal said. "Besides, they think the setting of a public high school will broaden the appeal."

Mom just shook her head. "I can't believe it."

"You sound like me, Mom. I've been saying that since I got in here," Abby said.

"The other thing that tipped the scale in her direction was the story—emotional eating, overcoming grief, a major move. We wrote about the cocoon in which Abby said she hid." Coach leaned over and put her arm across Abby's shoulders. "They loved the idea of helping the butterfly reemerge."

"So how do you feel about it, Abby?" Mom asked. "I'm all for it, if you want it."

Abby thought about it. How hard would it be to be weighed and measured on national television? And what about the huffing and puffing of her out-of-shape body as she tried to exercise? What if she couldn't stay on the diet? Would she be like Gloria from last season?

"Can I think about it for a few minutes?" She stood up. "Let me go get a drink of water. I'll be right back."

As she opened the door, she saw Damian craning his neck to see what might be going on in the room. Obviously word had already gotten around school about a strange meeting.

"Yo, Flabster, what's happening?"

Flabster. Abby turned around and walked back into the room without answering. From the look on Mom's face, she knew everyone had heard her nickname. "Forget the drink," she said, sitting back down. "I'm in."

"I knew you would be," Isabella said. "My mom said you'd love the proactive approach."

Proactive. That was Dad's word. "I'm still afraid I'll disappoint you, but I won't know if I don't try."

"Don't worry about that," Coach said. "We won't let you fail."

"At first we thought my mom would be the food coach, but Coach Mathews convinced me to do it. After all, I'm with you all the time." Isabella laughed. "Mom will be overseeing my coaching and will actually do the behind-the-scenes nutritional stuff, but I'll be the one who'll be your worst nightmare."

Abby laughed at the tough-guy face Isabella put on. "Sounds like we'll get to spend even more time together." Neither of them would mind that.

"So it's a go then?" the principal asked. "It's going to garner a nice little bit of publicity for Emerson. The school board should be delighted."

"And we can work out the girls' absences?" Coach asked.

"Yes. Luckily, most of the work will be done right here in San Francisco, right?" The principal jotted some notes on a pad of paper. "As soon as you know the schedule and the out-of-town filming dates, we'll work with their teachers on a few modules of independent study."

"As long as it won't impact Abby's academics," Mom said.

"We'll make sure it won't," Coach said.

All of a sudden, Abby thought of something. "Oh, no."

"What?" Isabella asked.

"What will we do about Cece's cooking?" Abby knew the pounds would never come off if she had to keep eating her grandmother's Sunset Sausage Simmer or Ten-Minute Shepherd's Pie.

Mom laughed at the blank look on the faces of the two women. "My mother's cooking is not what you'd call low-fat or low-carb or actually low-anything, for that matter."

"She's the queen of brand-name cuisine," Abby said. "She opens boxes and cans of prepared food by the dozens to create every meal."

"Guess what?" Coach said. "You don't even need to worry about that. It'll be Isabella's worry. She'll need to work with your grandmother on meal preparation."

For the first time since they entered the office, Isabella looked worried. "Me?"

Now it was Abby's turn to laugh.

"Don't worry. I'll help," Mom said. "The best thing is that Abby's grandmother loves her and will do anything for her, even if it means giving up her fifties-style cooking."

The meeting continued as they worked out logistics and schedules. Abby missed much of it. She couldn't stop thinking of the prayer she'd prayed all those weeks ago as she watched the footrace on *Less is More*. She still remembered asking God to help her find her way again. She knew she might not win any races, but she asked Him to help her at least get back in the running. *Thank You, Father, for answering my prayer. You know I can't do this on my own, but if there's one thing I've learned over the last year, it's that You stay beside me. I'm going to have to lean on You.* She thought for a moment before she added, *Thank You for letting Isabella be part of this. Let her see You in this process.*

"Where'd you go, Abby?" Coach asked. "We were talking about getting ready for the orientation trip."

"Sorry," Abby said. "I was just thinking about what an answer to prayer this is. And I mean a very specific answer to a very specific prayer."

Isabella's face showed the question she longed to ask, but she didn't say anything.

"Well, I was just saying that the schedule is tight," Coach said. "We'll actually begin filming the opening segment in two weeks, because they start airing the series the first week in January."

"So we start watching *Less is More* before the contestants are even finished with the whole challenge?" Mom asked.

"Yes," Coach Mathews said. "The producer believes it adds to the authenticity that when they air the opening segments, nobody could possibly know the ending, because the challenge is still in progress."

"Cool," Isabella said.

Abby wasn't so sure.

❋   ❋   ❋

"Destination?" The San Francisco airport skycap held his hand out for her ticket.

"Los Angeles," Abby said. Coach and Isabella were still getting luggage out of Mom's car.

"How many bags are you checking?"

"Just one."

"Are you traveling alone?"

"No. My teacher and my friend are traveling with me." Abby pointed to where they stood, manhandling their luggage.

"We'll get their luggage checked and put all the tags on one ticket." He went over and got the rest of the luggage, looked at their photo IDs, asked a few security questions, and finished the transaction. Coach handed a tip to him as he told them their gate number.

Mom looked concerned. She and Abby hadn't been apart for a single night since Dad had died.

"I'll be back in a little more than a week, Mom," Abby said, hugging her mother.

"I know. You are going to have a wonderful time." Mom kissed her and turned back toward the car. "Take care, Tracy and Isabella. I can't wait to watch this first episode on TV and see everything you will be doing."

Abby gave her mom one more hug.

"You will have a wonderful time. The fun part is that I get to see the whole thing on television later." Mom looked away. "I'd better get going before they tow my car away."

Coach and Isabella finished getting their luggage checked.

"Thanks, Karen," Coach said to Abby's mom. "I'll take good care of Abby."

Isabella laughed. "Are you kidding? We're going to starve her and work her to exhaustion."

"Well, that's heartening," Mom said as she got back into the car. She waved as she pulled away from the curb.

"Okay, girls, are we ready for this?" Coach asked.

"Ready," Isabella said.

"Can I go home?" Abby asked, only half kidding.

"Right after we go through security, let's get something to drink and go over our game plan. We've got lots of time." Coach led the way through the security checkpoint.

As they finally settled into seats at the restaurant, Coach said, "Tell us everything that worries you, Abby. Then you, Isabella."

"I don't know that I've put it into words, but . . . " Abby stopped to think for a minute. "I guess I worry most about failure. I've only ever had my weight creep up. I don't think I've ever really lost weight." She took a long breath in through her nostrils. "What if I can't do it?"

"You've got a valid concern, Abby. I'm not certain you can do it on your own either," Coach said.

"Right," Isabella added. "You have Coach and me, plus the support of your mom and my mom and, well . . . half the school at Emerson."

"That's right, but it's not what I was thinking," Coach said. "I was thinking of the verse that says, 'I can do everything through him who gives me strength.'"

"Right. Drawing on your higher power. Good," Isabella said.

Abby laughed. "I don't think Coach meant a generic sort of drawing on a generic sort of power."

Coach joined the laughter. "Abby's right. The whole higher-power thing is pretty loose and can mean almost anything. We need to add the power of prayer to our strategy and Jesus to our team."

Isabella thought for a minute. "Are we going to mention this on television?"

"I don't think we'll make a point of it unless it comes up naturally," Coach said. "Would it bother you?"

"I don't know. I mean, I'm all about science and the nutrition and exercise part of this. When we add a spiritual element, it's a little out of my comfort zone," Isabella said.

"I love how honest you are, Isabella," Abby said. "But I also love what Coach said. She's right. I know I can't do it on my own. I need that supernatural power."

"Will it make you uncomfortable if we pray together, Isabella?" Coach asked.

"I don't think so. I'm open to testing this out."

Abby smiled at her friend. "One of the reasons I said yes to this new adventure is that I prayed, asking God to help me make a breakthrough in this area of weight. When this came along, it already felt like an answer to prayer."

"Wow." Isabella paused. "I have to admit it's somewhat of a miracle they picked us, according to my mother. For one thing, you're a teenager, and dieting is controversial for teens, since many suffer from eating disorders already."

"I hadn't even thought of that when I applied," Coach said.

"I know. And then Mom says it's unusual they let Abby have what they're calling a hometown team. Professional trainers and nutritionists fight for positions on *Less is More.* Mom says it can make their careers."

Abby considered all that. "It's true; they may have just seen us as something out of the ordinary, but I think it looks more like the work of 'a higher power.'"

Isabella laughed. "Okay, okay. We'll use all the help we can get." She switched to her highbrow voice. "My professional reputation is on the line here. We've got to win."

"Let's pray right now and ask God to join our team; then we'll head down to the gate."

✳   ✳   ✳

"Welcome to your *Less is More* orientation. I'm Veronica Howard, producer of the show. I've already talked to all of you at some time or another." She looked trim in a pair of khaki slacks, a starched white cotton blouse, and a cocoa-colored cardigan. She wore a touch of lipstick and had her hair tied back—attractive but no fuss and no nonsense. She gestured toward Amy Leigh, the presenter and on-air personality. "I don't think Amy needs an introduction, since you've probably seen her on the show regularly."

Amy stood up. "I want to add my welcome. Y'all are in for a lot of fun over the next six months." Her Texas drawl and red hair made her seem that much more approachable.

"Okay, let's get started," Veronica said. "The first thing I want to do is briefly sketch intros of each contestant. You'll all have name tags, so it'll be easier for you to get to know each other. I'm not going to introduce team members, but in your breakout sessions you'll come to know each other better."

She held out her hand toward Abby and signaled for their team to stand up. "Our first team may be our most unusual team. This is Abigail Lewis. At sixteen, she's our youngest contestant yet. Besides emphasizing the youth angle, part of Abby's story will center on emotional eating. Abby lost her dad to a cardiac event just under a year ago. In the months that followed, her weight crept up." She signaled that they could sit down. "I know I said I wouldn't introduce team members yet, but Abby's team is equally unusual. Her trainer also happens to be her high school physical education instructor—the person who nominated her for the show. Abby's food coach is also sixteen and her best friend."

Murmurs rose from the room.

"Yes, it's our first amateur team, so to speak, but don't write them off just yet." She smiled. "Abby's food coach is Isabella Kazan, daughter of the renowned nutritionist Carol Kazan. Dr. Kazan's consultations will undoubtedly be available to her daughter."

An assistant came forward pushing a rack of clothing.

"As always, we will assign each team a color. This year, instead of the red team, the blue team, and so on, we're going for more descriptive names and more vibrant colors. Each contestant will get a whole range of workout gear in the team color, as will the trainer. Each food coach will receive matching lab coats."

The look on Isabella's face told Abby that her friend was much more excited about a lab coat than a whole wardrobe of workout gear.

"Our stylist considered the coloration of each

contestant and chose what we believe will be your most flattering color." Veronica went over to the rack and pulled out a deep pink. "Abby, yours will be the strawberry team."

"Cool," Abby whispered to Isabella.

Veronica went on to briefly introduce each contestant, calling him or her up to the front. Tajinder, Veronica explained, was a thirty-something mom who put on weight with each of her two pregnancies. With Tajinder, she said, they planned to talk about how a busy mother could still take time for fitness. When Veronica handed Tajinder the first workout outfit, Abby could see why they chose tangerine to compliment her olive complexion.

Veronica called up the next contestant. Bruce worked as an ad executive. His story would be about trying to lose weight in spite of a crazy schedule and lots of business meals and travel. Veronica handed him a pair of bike shorts in a color she called blueberry.

"All these food colors are making me hungry," Isabella whispered to Abby.

Veronica asked a middle-aged woman to stand. MaryAnn was a brand-new grandmother who'd let the pounds creep up over the years. With her they planned to focus on how to get fit over fifty. Her team received clothing in what Veronica called grape.

Veronica introduced Tanisha next. She owned a well-known restaurant in New Orleans. Tanisha loved to eat and could find no time to exercise. For her the stylist had chosen lemon to compliment her mocha skin.

"And last," Veronica said, "meet Dan. We're giving him lime to show off his wonderful tan." Dan was a carpenter whose weight had created a number of problems for him in his work.

"So each team will be identified by their color name—tangerine, lime, strawberry, and so on." Veronica looked at her clipboard. "Take note: one huge change this year. In the past we gave one large monetary award to the contestant who reached his or her goal first."

Veronica flipped a page over the top of her clipboard. "We discovered that was patently unfair, because men will always be first—muscle mass and all, you know."

Trainers and nutritionists nodded all across the room.

"This year we've found sponsors to offer awards for each team that reaches their goal by the end of the twenty-four weeks. After all, it can't be about comparisons and competition between the teams, since we have such different circumstances and even widely different goals."

A wave of discussion swept the room.

"Of course, every winning contestant will receive a makeover and new wardrobe as in the past. Each successful contestant and team member—including trainers and food coaches—will receive a brand-new car, along with ten thousand dollars cash."

MaryAnn—the grandmother—raised her hand. "That puts no small amount of pressure on us contestants, right?"

"It definitely ups the ante," Veronica said, smiling.

She looked at Abby and Isabella. "Because of the ages of Abby and Isabella and some liability issues, instead of a car, we've made an arrangement with a brand-new sponsor—a college testing service—to offer full-ride scholarships to both girls if they are successful. Their scholarships will be valid at whatever college each of them chooses and gains acceptance to. And, girls, you'll also get the ten thousand dollars if your goal is attained."

Abby couldn't believe it. That would be worth so much more than a car. Wait until Mom heard this. She grabbed Isabella's hand and squeezed. She just had to do this. *Please, God.*

"A few more details before we break for lunch. This afternoon we'll film the initial weigh-ins. Check the schedule for your time. Be sure to allow forty-five minutes for hair and makeup. When you are primped and ready, wait in the greenroom, and someone will come get you."

"Tomorrow, trainers and food coaches will work with our medical consultant to set the goal for each contestant." Veronica consulted her clipboard again, turning to her assistant to ask a question about the schedule.

"You can see that the rest of the week we'll be doing planning—food coaches will be together; trainers will also be together—and we'll be mapping out the segments."

Veronica handed a paper to Amy; then she spoke to the group again. "You'll be given a schedule for the traveling film crew. For every segment—every episode—we'll spend a day or two with each team in your individual hometowns. The only exception will be the two episodes that feature all six teams together. Those will be on location here. We'll let you know specifics later."

"Will the crew know what to shoot when they come to us?" one of the trainers asked.

"Either Amy or I will travel with them. I'll usually direct or plan the sequences, but Amy may step in from time to time. You don't need to worry—most of the filming will just be raw footage. We combine it to create a unified show here in the studio."

It sounded confusing. Abby knew she'd understand it better when they actually started.

"Okay," Veronica said, putting down her clipboard. "Let's go to the commissary and have lunch." She laughed. "It may be the last guilt-free food you contestants have."

Ready....

8

The soon-to-be-famous strawberry team had only been home twenty-four hours, but they knew they had to hit it immediately, even if it meant getting together early on a Saturday morning.

"This, fellow team members, is to be our command center," Coach said, swinging her open palm in an arc to include the entire girls' gym office and exercise room. "I've set up a special desk for Isabella over here."

"Cool," Isabella said. "Abby, can we get your grandmother to sew some strawberry-colored banners to hang over this area, so when we're on camera, we're even more colorful?"

"You guys are coming over for dinner tomorrow after church, right? Why don't we ask her then?" Abby wore her old sweats. She'd mainly save the new workout clothes for the on-camera time.

They had a week until the film crew came on Friday. Abby was glad. It gave her a little time to get used to the exercises so she didn't look quite so dorky. She spent way too much time wondering how she let herself get roped into this. She never liked being the center of attention, even when things were normal back in Suwanee. Now that her world had turned upside down and she'd let her weight get out of control, she'd be hauled front and center. How had she let this happen? Maybe it was just part of her cocoon thing—pulling back and letting others take the lead.

Not that she didn't love Isabella and Coach and what they were doing. They were putting their own lives on hold to help her with this challenge—she knew that. It's just that with this whole team focusing on her . . . was it real? Even if they prodded and pushed her into losing the weight, when they turned off the cameras, would she still be the same mess? Would she go back into old habits and be right back where she was right now?

Of course, the thing she worried about most was how she would come across on camera. She was glad they had this week before the crew got here. Maybe she could build up a little stamina in six days. How embarrassing would it be to do three sit-ups, only to collapse in a panting, heaving pile on the floor?

"Are you obsessing again?" Isabella asked her.

Abby nearly jumped. Sometimes it almost seemed as if Isabella could read her mind. "How'd you guess?"

"Let's talk about that first," Coach said. "It's natural for all of us to worry about this. I mean, I made the case for our team and pushed our proposal forward—first to the producer and then to the powers that be here at school. I hadn't expected the administrators and board to put quite so much stock in this, but they realize that it's Emerson High—their school—that will be featured every week this season. We may very well become the most famous high school in America this year." She laughed. "How's that for a little pressure?"

Isabella nodded, her face more serious than usual. "And for me, I've stuck my neck out here. It's only about fifteen months until I start applying for colleges. What if I'm a complete doofus on national television? Will any self-respecting science department take me seriously?"

Their confessions didn't lessen Abby's worries, but at least she wasn't the only one with concerns. She started laughing. "And here I thought it was all about those close-ups of my cottage-cheese thighs. What's wrong with us?"

"Let's go back to our motto," Coach said. "'I can do everything through Him who gives me strength.'" She pulled three chairs in a circle and waited while Abby and Isabella sat down. She sat last and bent over to rest her elbows on her knees, closing the circle even tighter. "What do you think about starting every session by remembering this verse and asking the Lord to be with us in this quest?"

"Good idea," Abby said. "It'll take a lot of the pressure off us. I know there's no way I can do this by my—"

A knock at the office door interrupted them. Parker

stuck his head in. "I heard you were back. Did you have a good time?"

"Hey, Parker," Isabella said. "We had the coolest time. The whole Hollywood scene plus lots of sight-seeing too."

"Looks like I interrupted a closed meeting."

Parker looked so good to Abby. She'd missed him while they were in Los Angeles. It felt as if one-third was missing from their friendship trio.

"We were just getting ready to get started on our planning session. Would you like to pull up a chair and pray with us before we kick you out?" Coach asked.

Parker laughed and explained that he had Saturday practice and wasn't planning on crashing their meeting. Still, he grabbed a chair, squeezing into their circle, and joined them in prayer.

"Want to come over for dinner tomorrow at Cece's?" Abby asked. "The whole strawberry team will be there."

"Strawberry team, huh? That makes me hungry already. Cece's, huh? Sure. I love your grandmother's cooking," he said as he headed out the door. "See you at church?"

They nodded, but as soon as he left, Isabella addressed a pressing problem. "What can we do about Cece's cooking? It's my first big hurdle in your nutritional planning."

"I don't know," Abby said. "I want this to be a success, but I'd give it all up before hurting Cece's feelings."

"I understand," Coach said, getting up from the circle, putting the chair back, and perching on the edge of the desk. She swung one leg. "Just as you admitted to being an emotional eater, your grandmother equates food and love. We need to be careful—she's been a rock of stability for you, hasn't she?"

Abby nodded.

"What if we don't do anything right away?" Isabella said. "When the camera crew comes the first time, let's feature a dinner at Cece's and use it as a teaching moment."

"Good idea," Coach said.

"As long as we don't hold her up to ridicule . . . I mean, use her as a bad example." Abby knew the pride Cece took in her cooking.

"No. We need to enlist her help," Coach said.

Abby thought about that. Interesting. Cece would be open to anything that would help her granddaughter. Abby knew that for sure.

"So what does Abby do for this first week then?" Isabella took notes as they talked. "We can't afford not to hit the ground running."

"As a start, I moved this refrigerator in here." Coach opened the door of the apartment-sized refrigerator to reveal bottles of water, fresh fruit, and vegetables. "Isabella told me that she's going to try to help you make good choices in a simple way instead of counting calories or going on a strict low-fat or low-carb regimen."

Isabella stood up, looking businesslike. Abby almost laughed but caught herself. Her friend would apply all her passion for good nutrition to Abby's quest. Friendship like that was nothing to be laughed at.

"Before I go into details on your new eating plan," Isabella said, "let's just say that you need to plan to eat breakfast and lunch here. For dinner, do the best you can until we get Cece to start cooking healthy."

Abby pictured some of Cece's dishes—like panfried corned-beef hash. "How do I do that?"

"Well, when I was trying to decide on a simple plan for losing weight, I considered one I would call the Half-Twice plan."

Abby didn't get it.

"Its simplicity is that you don't really change the foods you are eating; you just cut all the portions in half. If you normally ate a whole sandwich, you'd eat half."

"What about the 'twice' part?" Coach asked.

"Twice as much exercise." Isabella snapped her fingers. "Simple, huh?"

"It would work," Coach said. "Though I plan on a whole lot more than twice as much exercise."

Abby groaned. "So why aren't we going to use that?"

"I talked with my mom last night for a long time. She believes much of the food you've been eating is not adding much nutritionally, so by halving it, you'll lose weight, but you won't necessarily get healthier."

Abby could picture that half bag of potato chips vanishing from her life. "So I not only have to lose weight, but I also have to get healthier?"

Isabella gave her one of those one-eyebrow looks.

"Okay, so what will I be doing?"

"We're going to work on reprogramming your food choices to give you a lifelong eating plan. Instead of dieting, you'll just be choosing different foods."

"I'm guessing chocolate will not be on your hit list?" Abby said, batting her eyelashes, trying to look innocent. She had to keep this light, or she might break out in an anxiety attack right in front of them.

"Actually," Coach said, "you should be able to enjoy old favorites once in a while, right, Isabella?"

"Yep. And Mom says once you cut processed food out of your diet, much of the hunger and cravings will disappear."

"Really?" Abby had trouble believing this. Right now, thinking about a box of donuts practically consumed her. Too many times on the way to school she'd stopped at the donut store. Just sitting here at Emerson this morning made her want to go to her locker to see if a stray donut had somehow been overlooked. Habits might be her biggest enemy.

"Anyway . . . " Coach stood up. "Let's start you on your first day of exercise."

Abby felt tired already.

Coach explained the program, telling her that they'd move slowly so she could build up endurance without injury or too much soreness. "Overly sore muscles will make it hard for you to stick with the program for the initial break-in time."

Coach planned to use the weight bench and free weights, plus lots of contraptions with pulleys and weights.

When Abby squinted at the apparatuses—or was it apparati?—she could see their resemblance to ancient torture devices.

"But all that is just for muscle toning," Coach said. "We really want you to incorporate exercise as part of your normal life—movement that takes no machines or tools."

Okay, Abby had to admit she liked the plan so far— it was far less intimidating than she had feared. Commonsense eating and natural exercise. Maybe this *was* something she could keep up for a lifetime.

"We three will meet at your house every morning at 6:00 a.m.—" Coach didn't even get to finish her sentence because of the groans from both girls. "Oh, stop now."

"It's still dark at six. Dark and foggy," Abby wasn't sure still.

"But face it, girls—we have school in addition to this challenge, so we have to schedule tight."

Isabella rolled her eyes. "We'll just have to keep re-membering that full-ride scholarship, I guess."

"Good thinking," Coach said. "I'll swing by your house every morning at ten to six, Isabella. We'll drive over to Abby's and leave my car in the driveway. We'll take a brisk walk through the park, swinging in a loop so we can be back at the car by seven."

"A whole hour of walking?" Abby didn't mean for her voice to take on that whining tone. "I mean, I don't know if I can go that long."

"Probably not at first, but we'll work on it." Coach stood up and put an arm around her. "This is not going to be as hard as you think."

Abby had trouble believing that.

"Then, we'll get in the car and head to school. You'll do your weight routine for about a half an hour; then we'll eat breakfast right here, clean up for school, and be at our desks when the bell rings."

"So it'll all be done before school even starts?" Isabella asked.

"Uh-huh. I know you still have lives and families and homework. And even though I'm single, I'm not too ancient to maintain a social life myself."

The girls laughed. Coach was in her early thirties. They knew she had tons of friends. While they were in Los Angeles, the calls to her cell phone had shown that.

"Okay. So how do I start eating right?" Abby asked. Might as well hear the whole thing.

"Until we see how your body loses weight, I want you to follow these simple rules." Isabella put her finger up as if to count number one. "Don't eat anything that comes out of a package of any kind. That'll help you avoid processed food."

"What about bread?" Abby asked.

"Hmmm. If you are going to eat bread, let's get a high-fiber, whole-grain bread at the bakery." Isabella jotted a note on her paper. "Or ask Cece to make you some."

"Sounds yummier anyway," Abby said.

"Be stingy with fats; be generous with fruits and vegetables." Isabella put up her second and third fingers.

"Any more no-no's?" Abby asked. It almost seemed too easy.

"Try to avoid white."

"White?" What in the world was Isabella talking about?

"White as in sugar, white flour, white rice, potatoes, pasta." Isabella counted the five whites on her other hand.

"No pasta?" Abby loved pasta. If she couldn't have pasta, what would Cece put in those endless casseroles to sop up the soupy sauces and cheese?

"If you want to do pasta, choose whole-grain pasta. That way, all your carbohydrates come with rich nutrients and lots of fiber." Isabella looked at Abby. "Doesn't that sound easy enough?"

"Sure, as long as there's not a pan of brownies sitting in front of me," Abby said. "I'm a total loser when it comes to willpower."

"That's another thing we're going to prohibit," Coach said.

"Brownies?" Abby asked.

"No. Self-demeaning talk. You know what I think about the power of names. It's important to stay positive."

"But I didn't mean it bad." Though Abby said that stuff all the time to herself, she didn't mean for it to creep into conversation.

"Words have power, Abby." Coach paused. "As Christians we especially know that. After all, God spoke a word, and the universe came into being. And His Son is called the Word. Doesn't that indicate that words—and not just divine words—are important?"

"I know what you mean," Isabella said. "It's sort of like giving the words power by putting them out into the universe."

Coach smiled. "That sounds a little too new-age-y for me. I think it's more like one of my favorite Bible verses where it says, 'Whatever is true, whatever is noble, whatever is right, whatever is pure, whatever is lovely, whatever is admirable—if anything is excellent or praiseworthy—think about such things.'"

"Oh, I like that verse," Isabella said. "Where can I find that in the Bible?" She readied her pencil over her notebook.

Abby loved it that her friend had dug up an old Bible and started reading it. How like Isabella it was to dig into something wholeheartedly.

"I think it's Philippians 4:8," Coach said.

As they wound up their planning meeting, Abby began to worry again. Healthy food. Exercise. Good attitude. Could she do it all? Or would she end up letting everyone down and not only being humiliated, but humiliated on national television? *How in the world do I get myself into these things?*

Set...

9

Mmmm.

Mrs. Grady, this is so good." Parker took another bite of her French Onion Roast Beef. "I thought about your cooking all through the service today."

Mom laughed. "Better not tell Pastor."

"I didn't mean exclusively . . . " Parker grinned.

"I'm glad you like it," Cece said, smiling at him. "It's so easy. You just take a blade roast and put it in a baking bag with two packages of dry onion soup mix."

"Actually," Isabella said from across the

table, "this is not a bad choice for Abby." She took a bite. "It tastes good, but the choice of meat is naturally lean, and the onion mix flavors it with very few calories added."

"And these steamed green beans couldn't be better," Coach said.

"Karen—Abby's mom—explained that we are going to have to adopt a whole new way of cooking in order to help Abby with this challenge," Cece said. "I love quirky food and fun dishes—the same old stuff gets so boring, but"—Cece looked at Abby—"I love my Abigail more. I'm ready to join the team. Just tell me what to do."

Isabella smiled at her. "Abby's so lucky to have you in her life."

Cece laughed. "No, I'm the one who's blessed. Okay, what do we do?"

"For now, nothing." Isabella excused herself from the table and went over to her bag, taking out a three-ring binder. "I've put everything in here, but we won't start until next week. Abby's going to start making changes immediately at breakfast and lunch, but we'll leave dinner for now."

Isabella handed the binder to Cece. "We've decided to restrict carbohydrates to high-nutrient carbs and focus on fresh foods—prepared simply—or in the case of fruits and vegetables, eaten raw if possible."

Abby's mom jumped in before Cece could say anything. "That should be easy enough, Mom. And just think—you're going to have more time than ever for your garden. Maybe we can even grow some winter vegetables like Brussels sprouts, broccoli, or cabbage."

"And on the upside, since you won't be using

prepared food," Coach said, "the food budget should
go down."

Cece laughed. "I'm not so old that I can't tell when
I'm being handled. I can tell you have all been worrying
about my cooking. Don't worry; I'm going to practice
the old adage 'less is more' when it comes to cooking."
She patted the binder. "I plan to practically memorize
this thing, Isabella."

Abby looked at her grandmother. "Thank you, Cece.
You're the best."

"Speaking of you being the best, Mrs. Grady"—
Isabella tried to do her best wheedling, wide-eyed puppy-
dog look—"could we get you to make some panels or
banners of plain strawberry-colored fabric to hang in
the gym and Coach's office, so we can warm up the in-
stitutional look somewhat? My mom and dad may be
among the brightest practitioners in the San Francisco
medical community, but when it comes to making
stuff, they are all thumbs."

"I don't think we ought to spread the word that your
cardiac surgeon dad is all thumbs," Mom said.

Isabella laughed.

"No problem. I can make panels," said Cece. "I can
probably get acrylic felt—they have it in so many colors
this time of the year in preparation for Halloween
costume-making. Or maybe I should use polar fleece . . .
It would drape so nice. I'll take one of Abby's new
warm-ups to match the color."

"Thanks, Cece," Abby said.

"So the *Less is More* camera crew arrives Friday
morning?" Mom asked.

"Actually, they'll be here Thursday night so we can
start bright and early Friday morning. They plan to

meet us in time for our morning routine, then go to school, following Abby as she works out and makes her food choices," Coach said. "I just got an e-mail that they'll stay with us all day and go to the Bistro with us Friday night."

"Not the Bistro." Isabella groaned.

"Be fair, Isabella," Parker said as he forked another green bean. "You've never even been there."

"And I never wanted to go either," she replied.

"Looks like you have no choice," Coach said. "As Abby's food coach, you need to guide her through the pizza and brownie maze."

Isabella groaned. "I don't have to wear my lab coat in front of them all, do I?"

"Take it along. You may have to do an on-camera teaching moment, but I don't think you have to wear it the whole time," Coach said.

"Do we let Damian and Pastor Doug know?" Parker asked.

"No." Coach took another helping of green beans. "We want everyone to be natural, so we'll just let the crew show up."

"What about the . . . um . . . religious content?" Isabella's pause midsentence gave away her discomfort. "I mean, we shouldn't mix that in, right?"

"We'll let Veronica worry about what to include and what to keep out. It may all end up on the cutting-room floor," Coach said.

"Besides, the Bistro's more a social thing than a heavy-message-type thing," Abby said.

"No, I'm not worried about the faith message," Coach said. "I'm more concerned about what Damian calls his witty barbs. I don't know how that will look on camera."

"Well, if we can't tell anyone about the *Less is More* team coming, we'll just have to hope everyone's on their best behavior," Abby said.

"Good luck," Isabella mumbled.

"Friday night before going to the Bistro, we were wondering if we could have the team come here and film Abby at supper?" Coach asked Cece.

Cece pursed her lips. "You mean you want to feature one of my dinners as a 'before' moment?" Cece had watched the show enough to know how it worked.

Before Abby's mom could jump in to try to smooth things over, Coach answered, "Yes. You know how it's done, Elsie. They like to show a potential problem and then let the food coach do what they call a 'teachable moment.' Your way of cooking has always been homey and comfortable. Your family loves savory home-cooked food, and up until now, it's never been a problem."

She got up from the table to get a photo off the piano. It showed Cece beside Abby's grandpa, Mom and Dad, and Abby as a baby. "Look. Yours has been a family of naturally slim people or else naturally small eaters. The rich food you cooked didn't seem to affect anyone until Abby."

Abby put down her fork. How come she'd never realized that? What a loser—the only person in her family to have a weight problem. And now everyone had to change because of her.

Parker looked at Abby. "Just goes to show that God gives us unique challenges to help us grow."

He'd just come to her defense in such an encouraging

way. Could there be a nicer guy than Parker? "So what is your challenge, Parker?" Abby asked.

"Right now? Keeping from taking a third helping of meat."

Cece still hadn't said anything.

"So what do you think, Mom?" Abby's mother asked. "If you don't feel comfortable doing this, I know the team will find other 'before' shots."

"It'll be okay," she said in a voice that still sounded unsure. "I hate to think my cooking's caused Abby a problem, but if I can change it and help solve the problem, I can live with it."

"Your cooking did not cause Abby's weight gain. Don't worry that the team will focus on that," Coach said.

Abby hated for Cece to feel bad. "You should see the crumpled potato chip bags under my bed." She couldn't believe she'd just said that in front of Parker, but if Cece had to be real in front of the cameras, Abby would be real here as well.

"And that's just it," Coach said. "One of the reasons they chose Abby was because she's a classic case of the emotional eater. It's not just one thing that caused this weight gain."

"Sheesh," Abby said. "You guys are beginning to talk about me like I'm some kind of scientific case."

Everyone laughed.

"You're going to be so tired of being our guinea pig by the time this is done," Coach said.

"Abby, be sure to save those crumpled potato chip bags under the bed, okay?" Isabella said. "I can already see a cool teachable moment."

Abby crumpled her napkin and threw it at Isabella.

After dinner everyone left except for Isabella. The

girls planned to go on a walk once the food settled, but they couldn't resist kicking off their shoes and lying across Abby's bed.

Abby couldn't remember the last time she'd had a lazy Sunday afternoon with a friend. It was probably with Jen or Michelle before Dad died. She needed to e-mail Jen and Michelle and tell them about *Less is More*, but there'd been no time. That's how she knew she'd settled in here in San Francisco. Isabella seemed more real than Jen and Michelle. She still loved them, but she no longer wanted to just live in the past.

And it wasn't just her. Both of them had been taking longer and longer to answer her e-mails lately. She knew she was still important to them, but the deeper they got into school, the more that happened without her. It just took too long to catch up. She understood. She was the same way—how would she explain about Parker, Isabella, Damian, and the Bistro? It took more words than she had time to write.

"So are you excited about this whole challenge?" Isabella asked.

"I don't know." Abby tried to sort out her feelings. "It's scary to be at the center of all this. Sometimes I get afraid that too much is riding on me." She rolled over on her back. "What if the pressure causes me to revert to emotional eating instead of our new eating plan?"

"Have you felt like snacking or going back to your old habits?"

"Well, not so far, but we've only just gotten back, and we've sort of been caught up in all this."

"Maybe we need to have a plan for when it happens. If you begin to feel as if you'd give anything to binge, give me a call, okay?"

"I guess . . . but what would you do?"

"I don't really know yet, but I'll work on it. Maybe I should come up with some kind of emergency kit for you—a kind of don't-open-this-unless-desperate kit."

"Hmmm. Sounds like fun, actually."

"So what about the spiritual stuff Coach is always talking about? My dad was talking about new medical studies that have proved that prayer makes a difference in patient prognosis."

"Patient prognosis? I wish you'd speak English," Abby said as she elbowed her friend.

"It means how well sick people recover. They still haven't figured out why it works, but they do know scientifically that prayer works. Strange, huh?"

"It doesn't seem strange to me. The power lies in the person you're praying to, not in the act of prayer itself."

"Well, I find it interesting. I'd like to explore it more. I probably need to read about prayer in my Bible." Isabella went back to the problem at hand. "But do you think if you hit the wall dietwise, we could have some sort of prayer strategy?"

Abby couldn't believe this answer came from Isabella. *Father, forgive me. It took my skeptical friend to suggest the first line of defense. What's wrong with me?*

"Or do you think I shouldn't be praying, since I'm not really sold on God yet?"

"No. Luckily enough, we don't have to earn the right to be able to pray. Good thing, because if we did, I'd be out in the cold. Nope, you don't need any special beliefs or any secret code. The Bible says if we call on Him, He'll answer."

Isabella grabbed her pencil. "Where does it say that?"

"Don't ask me that. I'm terrible at knowing references." Abby rolled onto her side. "If I'm going to keep hanging with you, I guess I need to do a better job of studying my own Bible."

"So what do you think? Shall we make prayer our secret weapon?"

"I'll call if I start to crash and burn, and we can pray right over the phone." Abby knew her worst times were always while she was alone.

"I'm going to tell my father about this. I know he'll be interested in this experiment."

Ugh. More pressure. So I not only have the entire cable-viewing audience watching me try to lose weight, but Isabella and her family will be testing the effectiveness of prayer through my challenge. Abby could feel her jaw tightening. *Lord, help!*

Go!

10

Our cameraman is such a hoot," Veronica said as they met on the sidewalk outside Abby's house. "He's mounted a camera on the back of his trusty VW and will drive ahead of you as you walk. He's over on the path, waiting."

"I hope he got permission to drive the footpaths so we don't get arrested," Isabella said.

"No problem. There are so many films shot in San Francisco, they have a simple procedure for permissions and licenses."

"So we're ready?" Coach danced from one

foot to the other, doing her warm-ups. She wore the strawberry-colored warm-ups with the trainer insignia on them and the word *Trainer* embroidered across the back.

Abby wore one of her new workout sets as well. She stood waiting for instructions. She watched Coach deep-stretching with one leg out in front of the other. Forget warm-ups. She couldn't afford to waste one second of energy off camera. She'd be lucky to get one-third of the way before having to find a bench on which to collapse.

Isabella had borrowed one of Abby's strawberry outfits. It looked cute on her—a little big but definitely cute.

"This is a new experience," Veronica said. "We've never had a food coach actually work out with our contestant before."

"Is it okay?" Isabella asked.

"Of course it's okay." Veronica laughed. "I wonder if you are going to put a little pressure on our other food coaches. This should be fun. Tracy?" She called over to Coach. "Can you send me an e-mail on Monday and remind me to order workout gear for our energetic food coach as well?"

Abby slapped Isabella's hand in a high five and mouthed the word, "Score!"

Veronica took another look at Cece's house. "The cameras are going to love this old Victorian. Tonight's dinner should be a great segment for the first episode. Okay, let's head over to our rolling VW camera."

As they walked across the street, Isabella whispered to Abby, "Don't look so scared. It's a mounted camera, not a guillotine."

"A guillotine might be easier," Abby whispered back. "I can't believe I'm about to be shown to America in all of my out-of-shape glory."

"Time to employ our secret weapon," Isabella said as she grabbed Abby's hand. "God, please help Abby. She's nervous and worrying about looking good. She needs to just be herself and realize that even if she's not in good physical condition right now, it will help all those people watching who wonder if they can start a physical-conditioning program."

"Amen." Abby bit her lip to keep from laughing. It had sounded a little bit like Isabella was offering God a teachable moment. "You are such a good friend, Isabella. You remind me to be myself and to just be honest about where I am right now." Abby smiled. "Now that I think about it, if I was as physically fit as you and Coach, we would never have been chosen for the program."

They caught up to Coach and Veronica.

"Here's Dave, our cameraman. He's been driving through the park this morning and can't stop talking about how beautiful it is."

"We will get some gorgeous shots this morning," Dave said after introductions. "I love the interplay of fog and early morning light."

Veronica gave instructions. "Okay, just start your normal routine. Talk just like normal. We'll use parts that are interesting, but most will be edited out. This whole hour of walking will probably amount to less than two minutes on the episode." Veronica got into the passenger seat of the VW, and the walkers started out.

Abby thought about starting out vigorously, pumping her arms and looking like a serious walker. She could probably keep it up for about five minutes, and knowing they wouldn't use film from the whole miserable walk, she figured they'd get enough usable footage. But instead she thought about what Isabella had prayed. She started off at her normal snail's pace.

Coach and Isabella kept up their usual chatter as the walk began. Before five minutes had passed, Veronica turned around backward in her seat and stuck her head out the window. "Don't you ever talk, Abby?"

Abby didn't have enough air to laugh. "I can either talk," she huffed, "or I can walk." She waited to catch her breath. "But I can't do both at the same time."

Veronica clapped her hands. "Oh, I hope you got that, Dave," she said as she pulled her head in from the window.

They walked for about ten minutes more until they came to a bench. As the VW pulled out ahead of the walkers, Abby slumped onto the bench. "You guys go on," she wheezed. "Maybe no one will notice that one person's missing."

By that time, the VW had backed up, and Abby had a sinking feeling that the camera had caught her pathetic attempt at humor.

Veronica got out of the car. "You have no idea how refreshing you are, Abby. Too many contestants try to hide their 'before' shape and stamina." She sketched air quotes around the word *before*. "Without being able to observe your out-of-shape condition, the fitness you will eventually achieve makes no impact. "

"That's what Isabella prayed for me," Abby said. "She asked God to help me be real, so the viewers could see that sometimes it's tough to get started."

"Way to go, Isabella," Coach said. "It's like one of

my favorite sayings from C. S. Lewis. He said, 'Lay before Him what is in us, not what ought to be in us.' It's all about being real."

"You got all that, right, Dave?" Veronica went back toward the car. "Start again whenever you're ready," she said to Abby, Isabella, and Coach.

"Sheesh. I forgot they were filming," Abby said.

The camera crew followed Abby through her workout routine in the weight room and then breakfast with Coach and Isabella. Before they ate, Isabella donned her lab coat and talked a little bit about her philosophy of food—simple, fresh, avoiding prepared foods and overprocessed carbs.

When school started, the crew caught a few shots of students and lockers, but for the most part, Abby didn't see them again until lunch.

"Isn't it funny how many new best friends we have?" Isabella whispered to Abby as she put on her lab coat and they rushed to meet the camera crew at the cafeteria.

Abby laughed. She knew what Isabella meant. Word about the show and the film crew had spread around like wildfire. Kids kept crowding around Abby and Isabella, hoping to get on film. The school finally had to use one of the guards to keep a reasonable perimeter around the action.

As they walked into the cafeteria, Abby could see that Dave and Veronica were ready to go. Damian and the Bs stood just behind Dave. Damian watched without saying anything. She wondered if she should invite Damian to sit and eat with them, but she still didn't know him well enough to be sure he wouldn't upstage Isabella in some way. After all, this segment was all about food.

She saw Parker and waved him over. Parker she knew. "Join us for lunch," she said. She watched as Dave zoomed in. There. Jen and Michelle could finally see what the soon-to-be-famous Parker looked like when this episode aired.

"If I sit with you, I won't have to eat healthy stuff, right?" he asked.

Isabella laughed. "You're lucky you play football and train so hard. You can get away with a lot that we normal mortals can't."

Isabella turned to the camera. "We're fortunate here at Emerson High to have a salad bar. It gives us a whole array of healthy choices." She and Abby both took plates. "Today, Abby will make a chef salad for herself that will combine greens and vegetables with protein."

Isabella took the tongs and arranged a bed of lettuce on her plate. Abby followed her lead. Then Isabella added chopped ham, tomatoes, cucumbers, kidney beans, crumbled bacon, hard-boiled egg slices, and cubes of chicken breast. Abby did the same. Both girls chose their dressing.

"You'll notice that everything is fresh. We purposely ignored the diet dressings and instead used real dressing sparingly." Isabella looked into the camera again. "Specially prepared diet food can be a crutch. It's much better, in my opinion, to make real food choices that you can live with for a lifetime, rather than always having the mind-set of being on a diet."

Abby smiled. She could hear the words of Isabella's mother.

"And now we'll go over to the regular line and choose a piece of fruit. This is where Abby will satisfy her sweet tooth. Fructose, the sugar in fruit, is preferable to sucrose—regular sugar." Isabella sounded more and more like a teacher.

Abby chose a green apple. Fall always seemed like the perfect apple time.

"And as for something to drink, nothing beats water," Isabella said. "It's true that diet soft drinks have no calories, but if Abby can just get used to drinking water with every meal, she'll be taking in a portion of the eight glasses of water she needs to drink daily."

"Great . . . cut!" Veronica directed Dave to a different angle so he could take some shots of the friends eating in the cafeteria. "I like your common sense approach, Isabella. We have some food coaches using supplements, and others have the contestants counting calories, grams of fat or grams of carbs; others are weighing every crumb. It'll be interesting to see if your approach works."

"We're going to watch the weight loss and either add or subtract." Isabella took off her lab coat, folded it, and sat down next to Abby to eat.

When they stopped filming, Veronica came over and said, "We'll see you tonight at Abby's house for dinner. We're going out to get some San Francisco sourdough. Don't tell anyone."

As soon as they left, kids crowded in around Abby with a million questions. *Too weird.*

❋   ❋   ❋

The crew set up in Cece's living room. No one sat at the foot of the table. They left it open so Dave could wheel in for close-ups if needed.

"First, just eat and serve as you always do and talk like you normally do," Veronica said.

"Tracy, I'm so glad you and Isabella could come again," Cece said. "And Amy, welcome." Amy Leigh, the host of *Less is More,* had joined them for the dinner shots.

"Tonight I cooked one of my old standbys, Hamburger-Rama. My Fred loved this. Too bad Parker couldn't come tonight, Abby—he just loves my casseroles."

"Tell us how you made it, Cece," Isabella prompted.

"It's easy. First you fry up the hamburger, and then you add a package of dry spaghetti sauce mix—it comes in a little foil pouch. Then you add three quarters of a cup of water."

Abby had to smile. Cece was giving them an unforgettable "before" meal.

"Then you take a couple of cans of refrigerator biscuits. You just pop them open and press the biscuits into the casserole dish to form a crust. Then all you do is layer the hamburger mix, then add a layer of mozzarella cheese, then more hamburger mix, and then a layer of Parmesan cheese. You only have to bake it in a moderate oven for fifteen minutes and voilà! It's ready to serve."

The funny thing was that in spite of all the prepared ingredients and fat and carbs, Abby knew it tasted great.

"And this?" Coach asked, holding up a round dish with a crusty topping.

"That's my Spinach Surprise. Absolutely yummy and so easy. You just take a fourth of a stick of butter and melt it in a frying pan. You add two packages of frozen spinach and cook until they're thawed. Then you slice up a package of cream cheese—you know, one of those three-ounce packages—and you put that on top of the spinach to melt. You just add a package of onion soup mix and simmer it for fifteen minutes. Then all you have to do is put it in a casserole dish and top it with crushed corn chips."

Veronica stood to the side trying not to laugh out loud. Abby figured they thought Cece was laying it on thick, but actually the meal was not that different from every other meal she'd eaten at Cece's table.

Amy took a bite of her Hamburger-Rama first. Then she tried the Spinach Surprise. "Mmmm. I know I can feel my arteries clogging, but this tastes wonderful."

"No one in my family's ever had a problem with weight, so I never had to rethink my cooking until now," Cece said. "Abby's friend Isabella promised to help me simplify our meals and make them more healthy."

Isabella smiled. "Cece's such a wonderful cook; she's going to really help Abby. I know she's going to experiment with spices and flavorings and, in the end, will probably teach us about healthy cuisine."

Abby could see the smile on Cece's face. All the discomfort of Sunday disappeared, and she knew Cece was solidly in their corner.

Isabella talked to the camera a little bit about the wrong kinds of fats and the newest studies that highlighted worries over additives in packaged foods.

"And . . . cut," Veronica said.

"Okay, now that that's over, you and Dave pull up a chair and let me fix you a plate. It may be unhealthy, but it tastes so good." Cece still ruled her table.

"I love the shots I got in the house," Dave said. "Our viewers are going to fall in love with San Francisco."

"Let's eat then, and we'll head out to the Bistro," Veronica said.

＊   ＊   ＊

It took some organizing to get the team loaded up. They decided Coach, Abby, and Isabella would go first, and the team would show up about fifteen minutes into the meeting.

Parker must have arrived early, because when they walked in, he shouted from across the room, "What did Cece fix tonight?"

Abby couldn't stop laughing, but Isabella pretended it was a big secret and said, "You'll have to wait and see it on TV."

"Right on camera, Cece said she wished you were there," Abby said.

"See. You should have invited me."

"Are you still talking about your own personal film crew?" Damian's voice held a sarcastic tone.

"No, actually, we were talking about Parker's favorite cook," Isabella said.

"Don't tell me I have to put up with Isabella here at the Bistro as well as at school," Damian said.

"I know you think that's teasing, Damian," Coach said, "but it does not sound very welcoming."

Abby wondered if it really was teasing. Damian didn't answer Coach. He just moved off toward the head table and the Bistro Bs. Several more kids came, and the tables filled up.

Just as Damian stood to do the welcome, Veronica, Amy, and Dave came in.

"Yo, kiddos. Welcome to the Bistro. As most of you know, I'm Damian, better known as the Bistro Boss." He seemed to be playing toward the camera. "These young ladies are the Bistro Bs—we won't go into detail, since they're almost interchangeable."

Abby couldn't believe he said that. She caught the look of pain on Andrea's face before she covered it with a smile.

Isabella leaned in toward her and whispered, "And you think that makes people feel part of this supposed club?"

"You may have noticed some strangers here." Damian gestured toward Veronica, Amy, and Dave. "In case you've been living in an alternate universe and missed all the commotion at school, they're here as part of the television program *Less is More.*"

Come on. Turn the program over to Pastor Doug before you go too far, Damian. Abby's stomach grew tight. Damian seemed to have it in for her these days—ever since she turned down his food job.

"Why not have the star of the show come up and tell you about it? Let's give a big hand for the Flabster. Come on up."

Isabella started to stand, but Abby whispered, "Please, no. Let me handle it."

She went up, but before she started, Damian said, "Here at the Bistro, we're known for our nicknames. For Abigail we couldn't quite decide between the Flabster and Flabigail, but the former won out. Flabster?"

Abby looked out over the room. Coach crossed her arms across her chest. Parker looked uncomfortable, as did many others. "You can imagine how little I like that nickname. I'm so grateful for the opportunity to be a contestant on *Less is More.* As many of you know, my dad died about eight months ago, and it turned my world upside down. We moved here to try to escape the memories, at least for a time. When I got here, though, I sort of holed up in my room and stuffed my face. Food comforted me—"

"Well, thank you for sharing that, but we're getting close to TMI—too much information," Damian said.

Coach stepped forward. "No, we're not. You asked Abby to tell us all about it. Please give her the courtesy of letting her finish."

Damian sat down hard—almost as if someone pushed him down.

"Please continue, Abby," Coach said.

"I think getting picked for this show is a God-thing —a wonderful gift. Already, I've been able to discover some of the ways I hid from my grief." Abby looked out at her friends. "The reason I'm telling you all this is that I'm just starting on this journey. I want to be real. That means I need to ask you to pray for me, because this is going to be hard, and I'm definitely not up to this by myself."

Coach put an arm around her as Abby continued. "Isabella is the one who suggested we add prayer as our secret weapon. That's why I'm so glad Isabella is here tonight. She's not even positive she believes in God, but she's so open that she's reading her Bible and experimenting with prayer."

Pastor Doug came up. "I don't think I need to even add my words to yours tonight, Abby. I'll save my devotional for next week. Instead, let me just lead us in prayer for Abby. And anyone else who needs to begin a journey—whether it is a health quest like Abby's or a spiritual quest like Isabella's, let this prayer be for you as well."

Pastor Doug led the group in prayer, and at the end, he added a blessing for the food.

Damian stood up again. "Thanks for that word, Doug. Now it's time to get some food and enjoy the friendship to be found at the Bistro. You'll find video games, foosball, and all kinds of fun things, soooo, kid-dos, let the fun begin." He sounded back in control.

"Okay, Abby." Veronica came up behind her. "Are you ready to navigate your way through the goodies table for the camera? Then we'll get out of here and let you enjoy your friends."

"They don't all seem to be friends," Dave said.

"I don't know what's up with Damian. He's not usually so bad—"

Isabella snorted.

Dave began filming, carrying the camera on his shoulder.

"All right. Who knows? Let's go eat." Abby started toward the table and saw the usual fare: deep dish pizza, soft drinks, and for dessert, brownies topped with ice cream and chocolate sauce. She groaned and turned to Isabella. "So what do I do, boss?"

"You see the problem, don't you?" Isabella asked.

"Yep," Abby said. "Grease, white flour, and sugar."

"So could you just pass up the table entirely?" Isabella asked.

Abby looked at the brownies. "I guess so . . . "

"Be real. It's hard to do without when everyone is visiting and munching, right?"

"Right. So what do I do?"

Isabella whipped out a cute little metal lunch box studded with gaudy jewels—too cute. "You plan ahead. I brought this for you, just in case."

Abby opened the lunch box. Isabella had tucked a small wedge of angel food cake inside along with a pretty paper plate and a square of dark chocolate.

"Okay, take out the cake and put it on the plate." Isabella took the square of chocolate.

In less than a minute she came back with the piece of waxed paper on which she'd melted the chocolate in the microwave. She drizzled lines of chocolate over the cake. When she finished it looked like a work of art.

"So what do you think? Do you feel deprived?" Isabella asked.

"No, it's beautiful, but surely this can't be the stuff of diets."

"Actually, while angel food cake does have a good dose of carbs, it is low in fat, has no cholesterol, and is relatively low cal. That piece of cake is only about 142 calories. And when you're dying for a chocolate fix, dark chocolate is better than milk chocolate; and if you just garnish with chocolate, you're not doing that much damage."

Abby took a bite. "This is delicious. You've got to be the best food coach in the whole world."

Isabella looked right at the camera. "One other thing to note. I presented the dessert in an artful way— this time in a little bling-bling lunch box. Food is so much more appealing when it's presented with flair."

"And . . . cut." Veronica clapped her hands. "Isabella, you are a natural. Our viewers are going to eat you up." She turned to Dave and Amy. "Okay, let's boogie and let these kids have some fun."

"Good idea," Amy said. "If I stay here any longer, I may have to arm-wrestle Abby for that dessert."

As they left, Abby saw Damian standing off to the side, glaring at her. What was wrong with him? Somehow she knew she'd end up finding out.

Sore and Hungry

11

After the initial setup week, the strawberry team got down to business.
Cece began cooking the kind of meals that
made Isabella smile. Abby found her walking
distance increased a little bit every morning.
Mom even walked with them occasionally. She
enjoyed talking with Coach. It made Abby
happy to think that Mom had made a friend in
Coach as well. Back at the gym, Coach added
weight to the machines and upped Abby's repe-
titions. Things were moving along, and it was a
good thing, because the team was scheduled to

be back in three days for the official weigh-in. Cece's banners were hung, and the whole room had a festive air.

So why was it that when Abby woke up on Tuesday morning she could hardly get out of bed?

Mom finally came in at five thirty to see why she hadn't yet stirred.

"I'm sore, I'm tired, and I want a Krispy Kreme so bad I could almost kill for one." Abby rolled over and put the pillow over her head. "I don't want to play this game anymore. I want my old life back."

Mom sat on the side of her bed. "It's hard to stay focused over the long run, isn't it?" When Abby didn't answer, she left the room.

In less than a half hour, Coach and Isabella came into the room.

"I hear we have a rebellion of sorts," Coach said.

"I'm not sure if it's rebellion or not, but I'm worn to the bone today."

Isabella plopped on the bed beside her. "You're probably having a withdrawal of sorts—kind of like people do who give up caffeine. I read in one of Mom's books that when your body's making the change to a new way of eating it can cause a profound tiredness and symptoms almost like depression."

"I don't know what it is; I just know I want to stop having to be so regimented. I think I need a day to lie in bed and simply veg out."

"I'm going to go down and have a cup of coffee with your mom," Coach said. "You two talk it out, but be ready to go in twenty minutes."

"Now that's a feeling person," Abby said as Coach headed down the stairs.

"If you decide to throw a pity party on top of your rebellion, I'm out of here too." Isabella bounced on the bed a few times.

"But I really do feel awful. Do you think I have the flu?"

"No."

"What if I'm geting a cold?"

"A brisk walk won't hurt you, and who knows, once you get the blood moving you may be ready to rejoin the world."

Abby scooted down into the warm covers.

"Okay, I guess this calls for the secret weapon." Isabella bowed her head and folded her hands—almost like a little child learning to pray. "Dear God, it's Isabella again. I'm sorry I keep asking You for stuff when we barely know each other, but I'm asking on behalf of someone who's known You forever. She's feeling totally wiped out and discouraged—for no good reason. Help her draw on her reserves of strength. Remind her that since we already mentioned the prayer thing on camera, thousands, maybe millions of people will be watching the prayer experiment to see if prayer really works. I guess we sort of put You on the line here, God. Help Abby get up so she doesn't cause people to disbelieve—"

"No fair, Isabella. You're using spiritual blackmail. You know how much I love the Lord, and you're trying to make it sound like His whole existence is in jeopardy if I don't get out of bed."

Isabella laughed. "I didn't mean to make it sound like that."

Abby got up and went to the bathroom to clean up. *You have to love Isabella. Her praying is as honest as she is. Isabella has it backwards, though. We don't have to be perfect in order to show God's power. People seem to see God at work most clearly in our weaknesses, not our strengths.*

"Okay," she said to Isabella as she emerged from the bathroom. "I'm ready to pray now." She began, "God, I don't feel like moving a muscle. I want a donut. I want to stay in bed. I'm an emotional basket case. Take this mess and somehow make it a powerhouse. It'll take a near miracle, You know, because I don't have an ounce of reserve, but it won't be the first time You've breathed life into dry bones." She started to end her prayer but added, "I want to be an obedient daughter, so I'll take one step in obedience and get dressed. You need to take over from there."

She dressed and walked downstairs with Isabella.

"Good," Coach said. "You're ready."

They walked outside, and Abby soon found herself getting into the rhythm of movement—one foot in front of the other. *How much in life is like this? People only have to take the first step out of obedience and then lean on God to do the rest.*

By the time she got to school, they hit the workout room with enthusiasm.

"You know why you feel so much better now than you did when you woke up?" Isabella asked.

"Is it because I know I'm that much closer to waving good-bye to your cheery little self as you head off to your first-period class?"

"Okay, so the girl's still a little cranky." Isabella began stepping in time with her. "No, it's because of endorphins. When you exercise your body releases this stuff that makes you happy—gives you a sense of well-being."

"For real?"

152

"You can ask my mother. Remember back when we were talking about emotional eating? You can fight your emotional ups and downs with good nutrition and with exercise. It's really effective."

"I can't argue with you. I feel a whole lot better now. Much better than if I'd stayed in bed." Abby kept stepping. "I just wonder if it's endorphins or that God stepped in after we prayed."

"Or it could be a combination of spiritual and scientific—God stepped in and drenched you in a shower of endorphins."

Abby stopped and put a towel around her neck. "You're too much." She headed toward the shower. "Are you coming to the Bistro with us this week?"

"I don't know. I'm still having trouble with the whole thing. Last week, warning bells seemed to be going off in my head." Isabella walked with her to the shower. "I can't put my finger on it, but something is wrong there. I've been reading my Bible, and somehow the group doesn't seem to encourage us to be the kind of people God says to be . . . He tells us to be kind to each other. I don't think the leadership is very good at being kind."

"Damian, you mean? I think Parker is kind."

"Of course. I never think of Parker as leadership." Isabella looked at her watch. "Yikes, you'd better get your shower."

"Isabella," Abby asked, "how do you feel about Parker?"

"I'm crazy about him. Aren't you?"

"Yes, but in what way?" Abby couldn't believe where she was taking this conversation, but she felt she had to know.

Isabella looked at her for a minute. "Duh. I finally get what you're asking. Let me be clear—Parker is a friend, almost like a brother to me. I'm sure I'm the same to him and no more. There. Does that set your mind at ease enough so you can shower?"

Abby smiled. "It's not that there's anything between us, it's just that—"

"Yeah, yeah," she said while laughing at her friend. "Go take your shower. You're going to be late."

❋   ❋   ❋

Friday came, and the crew had come back into town to film the weigh-in and shoot most of the background shots they would need for the whole season.

Abby thanked God that He kept her going. The strawberry team did an unofficial weigh-in Thursday morning. Abby had lost seven whole pounds in the first two weeks. She weighed in at 166 pounds. Who'd have ever guessed that she could be proud of a weight like that?

"That's so exciting, but don't think that kind of weight loss will be repeated," Coach said. "The first weeks, the loss can be dramatic as your body loses the water it's been retaining. You probably don't realize it, but you've cut down drastically on salt intake."

"What is normal once it's not water weight?"

"I'll be thrilled if we can average two pounds a week."

Abby thought back to Gloria—the failed contestant from last season. *Please, God, be with me in this quest.* She was still wary of her emotions. More than once she'd nearly had a meltdown due to her emotions. The thing she noticed already was that her emotions were totally unreliable. When she felt fattest and just *knew* that she'd gained weight, Coach had her step on the scale. It shocked Abby to find out she'd lost. And just when she felt as if she'd never meet this challenge over the long run, she'd find herself making wise food choices that showed that she really did have staying power.

But she still worried about what she'd do once she didn't have her team around her. What if her success was really due to their strength and not her own?

Veronica and the team again met them at Abby's for the early morning walk.

"It's just going to be quick this time," Veronica said. "We want to show the progress you've made. We'll probably do a flashback to the segment before and contrast today's walk to show the growth."

Abby made it the whole way around their loop— not that she still didn't huff and puff, but the improvement showed.

"We'll probably get letters crying foul because you're so young and doing so well," Veronica said.

"You think I'm doing so well?" Abby asked. She could feel her cheeks flushed from the early morning exertion. "Wow, I'm glad. If you knew the struggles I've had."

"I'd like to put you on camera to talk about some of the struggles," Veronica said. "Dave, do you want to do some up-close interviews here in the park, or would you rather use an indoor setting?"

"Let's go with this. I love these California sunny fall days. Abby, if you sit on that bench over there . . . no, wait. Are you up to a hike back to the arboretum?" Dave asked.

Abby wasn't as tired as usual. "Sure." She elbowed Coach. "Especially if Coach will trade me the extra walking for less time in the weight room."

Coach laughed. "We'll have to, if we're going to be able to wrap up here and still get you girls to class on time."

Dave led the way with his VW. Coach took off walking with Veronica while Isabella and Abby followed.

"Okay, sit here," Dave said. "It's perfect. I love the way the light filters through the trees."

Veronica looked at the scene from a couple of angles. "Okay, I just want you to talk about some of the struggles you've overcome, Abby. Pause between thoughts so we have a good place to cut and splice in Amy's voice with appropriate questions."

"Is that how you always do interviews?" Isabella asked.

"Not always. It would work best if we could have Amy seated on the bench next to you, but we're spread a little thin—Amy and our other cameraman flew to Colorado to be with the lime team today. So we'll do this segment as a voice over. I may interject questions to take you in a new direction, but my voice will be edited out. It's amazing how it works—it's the magic of editing." She looked back to see Dave ready. "Okay, Abby. We're ready whenever."

"I've hit the wall more than once since I started the challenge." Abby felt funny talking solo to the camera, but she thought about how Isabella always did it. "One morning especially, I could have pulled the covers over my head and resigned from life."

"What made you continue?" Veronica asked.

"Strong-arm tactics. Not that I ever really had the

156

opportunity to quit, because my trainer and my food coach showed up for our morning routine and bullied me into getting out of bed." Abby paused and smiled. "The funny thing was that once I got dressed and began my routine, the quitting urge left me completely. My feeling of accomplishment banished all the aches and pains. My food coach talked about endorphins and exercise, but all I know is that it worked." She paused. She wished she knew how to work in the prayer part without making it sound preachy. Oh, well, later.

"The food cravings have been hard to deal with as well. I can't decide whether I'm really hungry for a particular thing or if it's just out of a sense of habit—just like a bowl of buttered popcorn always goes with a video movie on Saturday night. When you sit down to watch a movie with a handful of celery sticks, it's way too easy to feel sorry for yourself. I've found it's easier to give up the movie." She paused again. "I haven't really tested my own willpower since I have my food coach and my grandmother spoon-feeding me. I hope I'm making new habits and I'll learn to reach for different foods."

"Okay . . . cut. I think that's good. Lots of things our viewers can use. We'll either work those comments in here and there or we'll use it as a cameo interview." She talked to the whole team. "Okay, back at the school so we can do the weigh-in."

This time they didn't do any extra shots around the school, so it didn't take long to get the weigh-in segment. Coach talked about the problem of water weight on the first weigh-in, and Isabella talked about keeping the current food plan since it obviously worked. Once they had it, Veronica and Dave packed up and were out of there in time for the girls to start first period.

Segment one. As they would say in Hollywood—it was a wrap. Abby felt like celebrating; she was one-twelfth of the way through the challenge. So far, so good, but she wondered if she had enough oomph to do this eleven more times.

Less and More

12

December. How had time passed so fast? And as Abby sat down at her computer, she wondered how many months it had been since she e-mailed Jen and Michelle. Or Dad, for that matter.

"Dear Dad," she wrote, "I think you'd recognize me again. I've lost twenty-four pounds. Actually, I guess I weigh less than I did when you"—she paused—"when you went to heaven."

Almost a year hd passed, and that hot feeling still came to her when she thought about Dad being gone. "You'd think I'd be needing new clothes, but I'm just rediscovering my old Suwanee clothes. But next spring—that'll be another story. LOL.

"I still miss you. Not every minute of every day like at first, but there's still a big hole in my life. Funny thing, though . . . you know my friend Isabella? The one I told you about. She's still not a Christian but is in her Bible more than I am, and she's exploring the power of prayer. Well, her search has been bringing me closer to the Lord. Some of that hole left by your leaving has been filled with my heavenly Father." She took her hands off the keyboard for a minute, then typed, "I can almost see you smiling."

She took a deep breath. Her chest still hurt when she thought about Dad. "Both Mom and I have friends too. That helps. But don't ever think we'll forget about you." Abby's eyes filled with tears. "Love, Abby."

She hit Send.

Each week had proceeded pretty much like the one before. Abby did her best to follow the food plan set out by Isabella, and her loss seemed pretty steady. She read the chart on the wall. October 14th—seven pounds. October 28th—five pounds. November 11th— four-and-a-half pounds. November 25th—four pounds. December 9th—three-and-a-half pounds. Yep. Just like she told Dad, she was looking more like the old Georgia Abby. She wondered where she'd go from here.

The next weigh-in was the day after tomorrow back at the studio. Tomorrow they'd fly from San Francisco to LAX early in the morning and do the first on-location challenge in the afternoon. The next day would be individual weigh-ins and then a group recap.

❋　　　❋　　　❋

"It's so nice to have y'all here," Amy Leigh welcomed them while the camera rolled. "With very few exceptions, we're seeing a whole lot less of you."

Dan, the contestant from the lime team, shifted his weight from foot to foot. Apparently he'd struggled the most, and his loss barely showed. Abby felt so sorry for him. In the beginning she worried that she'd be the "Gloria" of this group.

"For our group challenge we have a surprise for y'all. In past seasons we've taken part in a footrace, climbed rock walls, and hiked Half Dome. Since this challenge is so close to Christmas, we've designed an extreme shopping trip for you . . . apologies to our men."

Everyone laughed.

"Here are maps with the route marked out. Each of you will be assigned ten top stores covering eight miles. You have a credit of one hundred dollars at each store to buy clothing and gifts. But just remember, you will need to carry your own packages on the whole route."

Some in the group groaned.

"Your trainers can accompany you—carrying water and helping you stay on course. You'll be happy that this is not a speed challenge but an endurance challenge." Amy smiled. "Everyone who completes the course with at least one purchase from all ten stores gets to keep his or her shopping spree."

After they turned the cameras off, most of the teams had questions. Veronica went over the instructions several times and handed maps out to the trainers.

"Is it okay if Isabella comes with us?" Abby asked.

"Of course. As long as you still carry everything and complete the whole route. Camera crews are set up along the route and at several of the stores. The most important thing is to have fun with this challenge."

The strawberry team started out.

"Can you believe I'm being challenged to shop?" Abby asked.

"For a teen, this is a piece of cake," Isabella said.

"Oh, don't say 'piece of cake'; I'm already hungry." Abby entered the first store—a kitchen store.

"It makes you wonder how much the stores had to pay to be included—just think of the exposure," Coach said.

"Who'd ever think of that besides you?" Isabella said. "I guess that's why Emerson is so happy to have the free exposure."

"Okay, you guys, I need to get something for Cece here. I hate to pick something just because it's light, but if I bought a marble cutting board, I know I'd never make it to the finish line."

"How about this lace tablecloth?" Isabella asked. "It's on sale, so you can afford it."

"Perfect." Abby took it up to the counter and made the transaction. "Can I have two of your shopping bags?"

The salesperson packed the cloth into the bottom of one bag and gave the other to her.

"Thanks. Now I'll just make sure I balance each thing with another, and no matter how wonderful, I won't get anything that can't fit in these bags."

It took the strawberry team four-and-a-half hours to complete the route. By the time they got back to the studio, Abby's arms ached, but her bags were full, and her Christmas shopping was finished. She'd never had the chance to be so extravagant. She made Coach stay out of one store while she shopped for her gift, and Isabella waited outside of another. Isabella helped her pick a gift for Parker—such fun.

One by one the teams straggled back. All of them completed the challenge except Dan and the blueberry team and MaryAnn and the grape team. Abby wondered if such a strenuous shopping trip was a fair challenge for a grandmother. Of course, not all grandmothers are created equal. Cece could do it and probably beat Abby's time.

The next morning they met for the group weigh-in. Abby's arms and back still ached, but she couldn't wait to go home and wrap gifts.

"Think *Rocky* when you run up to the scale for your weigh-in," Veronica said. "When this show airs, there'll be graphics on the screen to help the audience follow your loss. After you've weighed, step off the scale and stand next to Amy. Your team members should then run in and flank you. Got it?"

A few contestants asked questions, but the weigh-ins started. Abby couldn't help smiling. Twenty-eight-and-a half pounds. *Thank you, God.* When Coach and Isabella ran up to join her, they all laughed and hugged.

❋   ❋   ❋

After that triumphant first half, Abby wondered why the second half of the challenge started out so dreary.

"I'm getting a little tired of salads," Abby said as she and Isabella stood in line for lunch. Christmas vacation had been the hardest for Abby—too much time on her hands. If there'd been a bag of potato chips in the house, Abby would have consumed the whole thing.

Christmas without Dad—it was awful. Nothing was the same. Mom tried to do unusual things, like getting tickets for the *Nutcracker* on Christmas Eve, so they wouldn't compare it to last year, but it didn't really work.

Isabella's family invited them over for Christmas day, so that was different. Coach came along as well, since she wouldn't be going back East to her family until spring. Abby knew it would have been tons of fun had it been any other day, but, well . . . seeing Isabella's dad tease his daughter throughout dinner was almost more than she could take.

When she got home, she went up to her room and turned on her computer. "Daddy," she wrote, "I miss you so much it hurts. I guess on normal days I can stay busy enough to keep the loneliness pushed deep in my heart, but not today. I can't talk with Mom about it either, because I can see that today has been awful for her too." That familiar ache started in her throat, and her eyes stung with tears.

"I miss you. It's lousy having you gone."

She signed it, "I will always love you, Abby," and hit the Send button.

She thought about sending a Christmas e-mail to Jen or Michelle, but it had been so long since she'd e-mailed them, sending a Christmas e-mail would probably seem lame.

She checked her e-mail again and was surprised to find one had just come in. Who would send her an e-mail today?

No one. It was marked MailerDaemon@AmericasMart. com. The subject was "undeliverable mail." The e-mail she'd just sent to Dad came back with the explanation: "addressee unknown."

Abby put her head in her hands and let the tears flow. She'd never felt so defeated. So alone. How she wished she had a drawer full of chocolate . . . something. She put on her coat.

"I'm going out for a walk," she yelled to Cece and Mom as she walked out the door. She decided to walk to Starbucks for a Caramel Macchiato and a brownie. Starbucks should be open even though it was Christmas because of all the Jewish people in the neighborhood. She could have called Coach or Isabella to help her make a better food choice, but at this point, she didn't care. Addressee unknown. Is that what happened when someone died? They just started disappearing bit by bit?

She ordered her drink and dessert and took it to a table in the corner. Just as she bit into her brownie, she looked up to see Damian sitting at another table by himself.

"Yo, Flabster!" He waved at her. "What in the world are you eating?"

Why did he always have to talk so loudly? She didn't bother to answer, but that didn't stop him. He came over and sat down at her table.

"So, we eat light at Christmas dinner and pig out in private?" He laughed. "Wait until this gets around."

"Damian, go pick on somebody else. I'm not in the mood." She took a drink. She wished she could say that it didn't taste that good, but it did.

"So why are you all alone on Christmas?"

"Why are you?" Abby didn't intend to be mean, but she wanted to be left alone.

"I hate Christmas."

Now he had Abby's attention. She put her brownie down. "Why do you hate Christmas?"

"My mom left us right before Christmas one year. Just walked out. My dad can't stomach the season, so he uses it for political posturing—serving at soup kitchens right in front of the cameras." He shook his head as if to clear it. "Don't let me be a downer."

Abby had never seen him open up before. Maybe his put-downs were a way of dealing with his own emotions.

"Thanks for sharing that, Damian," she said. "I'm feeling pretty down as well. This is my first Christmas without my dad. It's my first Christmas away from home too. I came here to drown my sorrows in chocolate and calories."

"Sorry for calling you Flabster. It seemed like fun when I started, and now it's kind of expected. Everyone looks to me to be the funny guy. It's a heavy responsibility," he said, grinning, "but somebody's got to do it."

"Hey, Abby, Damian." Parker walked in.

"I called to say Merry Christmas, Abby, and your mom said you went out for a walk." Parker pulled out a chair and sat down. "She sounded a little worried, so I decided to take a walk myself and see if I came across you."

Maybe she wasn't as alone as she felt. It wasn't Dad, but having friends . . .

"I'm going to boogie, kiddos. I think I'm going to fix something yummy for my little brother," Damian said.

"Thanks for talking to me, Damian," Abby said.

"No prob." He waved as he walked out the door.

"Thank you for the beautiful Christmas gift, Abby. A

hardcover set of *The Chronicles of Narnia*—I could hardly believe it."

"Well, you know about my shopping trip. I'm just glad the bookstore was last on my itinerary. I could never have carried them the whole way."

"It means so much to me." Parker took her hand and held it. "Thank you."

Abby felt a little funny. Good funny, but funny all the same. "Since you came to rescue me, how about eating this brownie and drinking my drink. You are just what I needed—a friend to save me from an emotional eating binge."

He laughed and took the brownie and drink. "It's been a tough Christmas, hasn't it?"

"I may get through it with the help of friends." She meant it too.

❋   ❋   ❋

Yes, the month of December had its dreary moments. January had finally come—not that winter in San Francisco felt that much different than fall. Abby was glad when school started again.

"This is a good day to decide you're tired of salads," Isabella said as they stood in line. "They've added veggie wraps to the lunch menu. Do you think it could be my influence? Whole wheat tortillas and roasted vegetables and cream cheese—yum."

"Are you going to the Bistro tonight?" Abby asked.

"I'd rather not. I'm still not enjoying it. Last week it seemed like even more kids were joining the leadership team with the put-downs and jokes." Isabella chose a pear to go with her wrap. "I guess I'm just not cool. Or maybe it's because I'm an only child and haven't had brothers or sisters to torture me . . . "

"I think Coach planned to finally talk to Pastor Doug about it this week. Maybe they'll come up with something." Abby grabbed a bottle of water and followed Isabella to the pay station. "I just like it so much better when you're there with me."

"All right. I'll give it another try." She paid and turned back to Abby. "I'm going to try to focus on Pastor Doug and the other kids this time."

When they got there, the talk was all about *Less is More*. The first episode was to air next Thursday night—just in time for all those who made New Year's resolutions. Everyone wondered if they'd make it on the show. The crew had filmed on campus and at the Bistro.

Abby and Isabella sat down next to Ashley. "Where's Parker?" Abby asked.

"He's giving the meditation tonight since Pastor Doug couldn't make it, so he's probably pacing."

Damian opened the meeting with the same fast-paced, fast-talking style, but Abby knew she would never see him in the same light again.

As Parker got up to give the meditation, Abby saw that he was using one of the books she had given him for Christmas. Isabella poked her.

"Tonight, I wanted to read you a short passage from one of my favorite books, *The Voyage of the Dawn Treader*. It's one of *The Chronicles of Narnia* by C. S. Lewis. I'd like to tell you a little bit from the story of the undragoning of Eustace."

"First some backstory. Eustace was a terrible boy—selfish and dull. Throughout this voyage of enchantment he irritated everyone with his know-it-all ways.

He ended up, through a series of events, being turned into a dragon . . . You'll need to read the book; it's so descriptive," Parker said.

"His friends discovered that due to the misery of being a dragon, Eustace became someone they could begin to like, although no one could help him break the enchantment and become a boy again. After nearly giving up hope, Eustace, the boy, appeared again with the tale of how he'd been undragoned." Parker paused. "This is the part I love, because we all have dragons of some kind or another from which we need to be freed."

Abby settled in to listen.

"Eustace told how the lion Aslan—and you all know Aslan is the Christ-figure in these books, don't you?— Aslan came to Eustace and took him to a well. Eustace's arm ached from a gold band constricting it, and he longed to crawl into the well and cool his throbbing pain, but Aslan told him he must undress first." Parker laughed. "For some reason this made sense to Eustace —like a snake shedding its skin. So he clawed at himself until he clawed a complete skin of scales off. As he went to step into the water, he noticed he had another skin of scales under that one. He clawed again and removed that skin. He said it didn't really hurt that much, but underneath he found another dragon skin. He repeated this a third time and the same thing happened. He was no closer to having his real skin revealed."

Abby looked around and saw that everyone listened.

"Aslan said, 'I must undress you.' By this time Eustace was desperate, and he lay flat so that Aslan could undress him, despite his being frightened of the lion's claws. Eustace said that the very first tear was so deep he thought it sunk into his very heart. It hurt worse than anything Eustace had ever felt."

Parker opened the book. "Let me read this from the book. 'Well, he peeled the beastly stuff right off—just as I'd thought I'd done myself the other three times, only they hadn't hurt—and there it was, lying on the grass: only so much thicker, and darker, and more knobbly-looking than the others had been. And there was I as smooth and soft as a peeled switch and smaller than I had been.'"

Parker closed the book. "I've been thinking about Abby and her *Less is More* adventure."

Damian made a face and gave a whistle—as if to tease Parker for thinking about Abby.

Parker ignored him. "As we've watched Abby's transformation in progress, it made me think of those ugly, dragonlike skins we all wear." He smiled. "That is not to say your skin was ever ugly, Abby—and I'm not talking about literal skin here either."

Abby smiled. She understood where Parker was going with this. She'd never thought of her transformation mirroring a spiritual transformation, but that had been happening as well. The more she leaned on the Lord, the more she came to know Him.

"I guess when I read the part about Eustace being smaller after Aslan undragoned him, it made me think of the concept *Less is More.* But thinking in terms of the spiritual—which is more important than the physical—it's like John 3:30 says: 'He must become greater; I must become less.'"

Parker shrugged his shoulders. "So that's what I've been thinking about. Like Eustace, we can let God work on us to cut through our self-centeredness. It might hurt to have the Lord dig deep enough to undragon us, but less of us leaves room for more of Him and His goodness. Less is more. I'm praying that we all seek a deeper transformation."

Damian stood up. "Interesting. Dragons and lions and ripping claws. Let's eat." Coach came forward and prayed, and then everyone moved toward the food.

Isabella seemed unusually quiet. When Parker came up, she put a hand on his arm and said, "I love what you said. I'm beginning to see how all of this ties together. This Christianity is simple on the surface but deep enough to keep us engaged for eternity, isn't it?"

Abby almost forgot to breathe. It sounded like Isabella was ready to make a decision to follow Christ. *Lord, please, continue to draw her toward You.* As they moved toward the food, Abby automatically reached for a cookie.

"No, Abby," Isabella said. "What are you thinking?"

Abby laughed. "I got so caught up in what you were saying, I reverted."

"Hold the phone," Damian yelled. "I have another nickname." He walked over to Isabella.

No! Abby couldn't believe Damian was so insensitive. Not tonight of all nights when Isabella was so close to putting her trust in God.

"I'm not a fan of nicknames," Isabella said to Damian, moving away from him.

"Are you saying *no?*" he asked. "If so, I have the perfect nickname for you. Listen up, everyone. I heard Isabella tell Abby no and practically slap her hand." He paused, drawing it out.

Abby saw red creeping up Isabella's face.

"We've all seen Isabella running around in her lab

coat, right?" He waited until several kids nodded their heads. "Her new nickname is . . . Dr. No. Is that perfect or what?"

Abby heard a sound coming from Isabella, as if she might cry, before she turned and ran out of the room.

Coach came over to Abby. "What happened?"

Abby told her and added, "And I think she was on the verge of accepting Christ." Abby felt like crying too. "Come on, Parker, let's go find her so she doesn't walk home alone."

A New Challenge

13

Isabella refused to talk about the Bistro and said she was not coming back. And Isabella never mentioned her interest in making a decision about the claims of Christ.

An amazing thing happened on the Thursday of the opening show. Pastor Doug called to ask if he could show parts of it at the Bistro the next evening. Abby decided to let him go ahead. After all, much of America had already seen it. At this point, she had little to hide. Abby wondered if Isabella would come.

"Cute outfit," Isabella said, coming up behind her in the cafeteria.

"It's a good thing I'm getting some new clothes. Less and less is fitting me."

"That's not such a bad problem to have, is it?" Isabella didn't have to guide Abby's food choices much anymore. Her new eating had become natural. She felt healthier than she'd been in a long time.

"Will you consider coming to the Bistro with Coach and me tonight—"

"Are you kidding?" Isabella's tone spoke volumes.

"It's just that Pastor Doug called and asked if he could feature a few clips from *Less is More*. I thought it would be fun to have the whole team there." Abby knew she was babbling. "Besides, it's more fun when you're there."

"Abby, I didn't exactly leave gracefully last week."

"It doesn't matter. You'll be with me and Coach and Parker and Ashley—"

"All right. All right."

Abby didn't dare say another word, but she kept praying that nothing bad would happen.

❋ ❋ ❋

"We're using the data projector," Pastor Doug said, "so you can all see our stars bigger than life."

Abby smiled—sort of. Hopefully, the camera hadn't caught any particularly bad zit days.

"If you want to get snacks now, you can munch while you watch." Pastor waited until everyone got food, then he finally said, "Okay, let's watch."

He opened on the segment of her sitting in front of

the arboretum. She talked about how tough the challenge was. The camera angle, the background sounds—everything made it much more effective than if they'd done straight shots. Abby felt self-conscious sitting there in the Bistro having everyone watch her deepest musings.

Following that close-up, the scene switched to the Bistro. Some of the kids hooted as they saw themselves on the screen. Then the scene switched to a quiet interview with Abby where she told how difficult it was to be an overweight person in a world that worshiped the thin and beautiful.

"Thought-provoking, Abby," Isabella whispered.

The scene switched back to the Bistro and focused in close on Damian as he said, "Why not have the star of the show come up and tell you about it? Let's give a big hand for the Flabster. Come on up."

Pastor Doug shut the projector off. "I thought it was important for us to see what we look like." He opened his Bible. "Let me read you a passage from the Bible," he said.

"Wow, the Bistro's way different tonight," Isabella whispered.

"I'm reading from Matthew 12:33–37." He cleared his throat. "'Make a tree good and its fruit will be good, or make a tree bad and its fruit will be bad, for a tree is recognized by its fruit. You brood of vipers, how can you who are evil say anything good? For out of the overflow of the heart the mouth speaks. The good man brings good things out of the good stored up in him, and the evil man brings evil things out of the evil stored up in him. But I tell you that men will have to give account on the day of judgment for every careless word they have spoken. For by your words you will be acquitted, and by your words you will be condemned.'"

Isabella's eyes got big.

"Those are powerful words," Pastor Doug said. "And they are the words of Jesus."

The room seemed unusually quiet.

"We've talked about the importance of names before and of the power of words, but it's been brought to my attention lately by more than one person that the name-calling here in our group is out of hand. I think the video showed us what it looks like from the outside in."

Damian sat with his head down.

"And don't think it's only Damian, by the way." He moved over to put an arm across Damian's shoulder. "He may have been caught on tape, but we've all been guilty of letting our words run away from us. I should have stepped in before things went this far."

Because of what Abby knew about Damian, she knew this must be difficult for him in spite of Pastor Doug sharing the blame. Damian had been hiding behind his wit and his barbs, but deep down he was just another lonely kid in need of approval.

"I'm going to ask Coach Mathews to come up here," Pastor Doug said.

She walked up to the front and stood leaning against the leadership table. "You've all watched us with our *Less is More* fitness challenge," Coach said. "It's been such fun, and you've all seen the transformation in Abby."

Abby still squirmed at being used as an example in front of her peers.

"Now it's your turn. I'm going to issue a fitness challenge for all of you, and the reward will be much more valuable than even Abby's prize."

The sounds of whispers swept across the room. Isabella looked at Abby with that quirked eyebrow, as if to ask what Coach was up to.

"I have a sign-up book here, if you're willing to accept the challenge." Coach smiled.

"But what's the challenge?" Ashley asked.

"I thought you'd never ask. We are embarking on a Spiritual Fitness Quest. It's like the story Parker told all those weeks ago. It's high time we undragon ourselves and get real. Remember the C. S. Lewis saying I quoted on *Less is More?* 'Lay before Him what is in us, not what ought to be in us.'"

"I'm going to be your trainer," Coach said. "Each week we'll have a new challenge—something to think about." She opened the book and laid a pen beside it. "So I'm challenging you. This week we saw the destructive power of put-downs and sarcasm. I'm asking you to take a pledge to rid your language of these negatives. Who wants to take the pledge?"

A group of kids, including Parker and Abby, came forward to sign up. As the line dwindled, Damian stepped down from the head table. "I know you said we all need this challenge, but I saw that video, and I'm ashamed." His voice shook. "Will you all forgive me? I didn't know how it looked. I mean, I was trying to be the life of the party—to keep things hopping—and all the time, I was . . . well, I don't know what I was doing, but it sounded awful when I heard it played back."

Parker came over and stood next to Damian.

"Abby, will you forgive me?" Damian asked. "And Isabella—especially Isabella—you saw it from the first, didn't you?" He shook his head. "Will you all forgive me?"

"Damian, it's not just you," Coach said, "though your repentance is a powerful evidence of God's work in your life."

The meeting broke up soon after that. As Parker, Abby, and Isabella walked home, Isabella opened the subject. "Seeing the change in Damian—from arrogant to humble and honest—makes me understand the power of faith. It's like you said all those months ago, Abby, that church is not a museum for saints but a hospital for sinners."

"Yep, but people just don't get that," Abby said. "They think we need to be good before God accepts us."

"Well, seeing Damian softening really shows God's power, not the power of religion or ideas."

"So have you decided to follow Christ?" Parker asked.

Abby hadn't expected such a direct approach.

"I have. It seems like once you make the decision to seek Him, you're a goner," Isabella said, laughing.

Abby hugged her. "I'm so glad you made the decision, especially since I know you. You never do things halfway."

❄   ❄   ❄

The *Less is More* challenge churned on. With the help of Coach and Isabella, Abby stayed on track for the most part. She had a setback in February, near the anniversary of Dad's death, but she recognized the emotional upheaval and resisted the urge to drown her feelings in food.

The weight kept coming off—not in huge numbers but steady numbers. By the weigh-in on February 24th, she was 129 pounds. She had four weeks and only four pounds to go. The strawberry team was pretty sure that they'd be celebrating her success.

The episodes were airing, and ratings for the series were great. Abby got a kick out of the fan mail she'd already received. This week's episode had featured more of the background stuff about Abby's struggle and focused on the strawberry team.

Before they knew it, Abby, Coach, and Isabella triumphantly headed down to Los Angeles to film the final segment. In this season, all the teams made their goal except for Dan's lime team. And even at that, he'd lost about half of his goal amount and was looking much better.

Abby had her final makeover, and the *Less is More* team surprised Coach and Isabella with makeovers as well.

"Look at me," Abby said, pirouetting in front of the mirror. "I can hardly believe it—125 pounds." She reached out to hug her friends. "Thank you both. I worried that I'd never be able to keep it up without you, but you're such good coaches that eating healthy has become a habit."

"Well, we're all looking pretty good," Isabella said. "Has this been fun or what?"

"It's been fun; it's been exhausting; it's been scary; it's been wonderful . . ." Coach paused. "I'm so glad I got to know you both. Despite the age difference and the teacher-student thing, we've become friends."

"Maybe the best part of all," Abby said, "has been the spiritual part. Isabella went about prayer in such a scientific way that she taught me to pray my way through tough things."

"Okay, let's go do the final weigh-in," Isabella said.

As Abby got on the scale, she wished Mom and Cece could be there. She always felt Dad was close by. And she wished Parker were there. To her the day represented so much more than successfully completing the weight-loss challenge. She had had no idea when she started this that her weight change would be the least of her changes.

Thank You, God, for not only answering my cry for help, but for taking me so much further. You really did give me the strength I needed. Continue to help me—not just me, but the whole Bistro crowd with our Spiritual Fitness Quest.

The final weigh-in was festive—colors flying and music playing. With great fanfare the checks, cars, and scholarships were awarded. Abby had no trouble smiling for the camera. She had already received the best prize of all—she had not only emerged from her cocoon; she'd found her wings.

Real TV series

Olivia O'Donnell wins a total fashion makeover on the hot new reality TV show *Changing Faces*. After her whirlwind trip to Hollywood, she comes home sporting a polished, uptown look. But as she deals with her overcommitted schedule and the changed attitudes of those around her, she has to face the fact that her polish is only skin deep.

Changing Faces
ISBN: 0-8024-5413-5
ISBN-13: 978-0-8024-5413-3

Best friends Chickie and Briana know everything about each other—or so Chickie thinks. But when they win a spot on the reality TV show *Flip Flop,* Briana is terrified people will find out her shocking family secret. Both girls get more than the makeover of their bedrooms, they learn a lesson in how to trust God for the makeover of their homes and not-so-perfect families.

Flip Flop
ISBN: 0-8024-5414-3
ISBN-13: 978-0-8024-5414-0

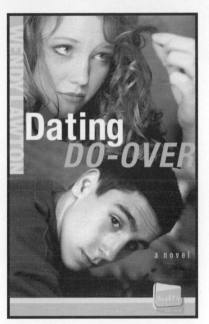

MOODY
PUBLISHERS

THE NAME YOU CAN TRUST®

LESS IS MORE TEAM

ACQUIRING EDITOR
Andy McGuire

COPY EDITOR
Ali Childers

BACK COVER COPY
Laura Pokrzywa

COVER DESIGN
UDG DesignWorks
www.thedesignworksgroup.com

COVER PHOTO
Photodisc

INTERIOR DESIGN
BlueFrog Design

PRINTING AND BINDING
Bethany Press International

The typeface for the text of this book is
Giovanni